By Hook or by Rook

More from Phase Publishing
by
Rebecca Connolly

The Arrangements
An Arrangement of Sorts
Married to the Marquess
Secrets of a Spinster

The London League
The Lady and the Gent
A Rogue About Town
A Tip of the Cap

Coming Soon
Fall from Trace

The Spinster Chronicles
The Merry Lives of Spinsters
The Spinster and I
Spinster and Spice

By Hook or by Rook

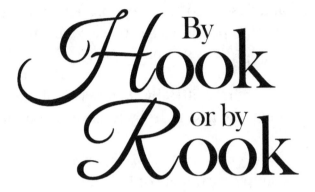

Rebecca Connolly

Phase Publishing, LLC
Seattle

Phase Publishing, LLC first paperback edition
July 2019

ISBN 978-1-943048-84-7
Library of Congress Control Number 2019943430
Cataloging-in-Publication Data on file.

*A*cknowledgements

To all my supporting characters who come alive with such vivacity that I have no choice but to write a full story for them, as well. Y'all are sneaky and know just where to get me, but I love you. And in some cases, your stories wind up being favorites anyway.

And to popcorn, in all its magical varieties, for being the most perfect snack and such a delightful addition to any particular moment. Let's make this thing official and go long-term, okay?

Want to hear about future releases and upcoming events for Rebecca Connolly?

Sign up for the monthly Wit and Whimsy at:

www.rebeccaconnolly.com

Chapter One
London, 1825

"*I* need a favor."

Jeremy Pratt hated those words more than perhaps any others in the English language. It typically did not bode well for him to be on the receiving end of such a thing, and it was never a good thing when the favors came at the behest of his colleagues.

One of the many hazards of being a covert operative for the Crown.

Given that they were all elbow deep in reports, notes, projects, and a sudden increase in activity by the traitors they monitored, it was a very poor time for favors to be requested. And that was just the work that Jeremy was doing officially for the League. It didn't consider his private investigation, ongoing for several months now, which he took up at every available opportunity, robbed him of his sleep, and constantly turned over in his mind.

And there was also his public life to maintain.

Mr. Jeremy Pratt was a fop in every respect, but the sort that charmed in a rather roguish way. He was popular and sought after, envied and emulated, and everybody wanted to see and know what he would do next. It was the best cover he had ever had in his life, playing everything to the extreme and being thought sillier than he'd ever manage to be on his own.

It was astonishing how little credit anyone gave such a man, and Jeremy used their ignorance to his advantage. There was always so much to see and do without anyone suspecting him. Dancing the night away and then sneaking back into residences long after the flamboyant Mr. Pratt had been seen making his grand exit; eavesdropping on private conversations while pretending to have fallen asleep in a parlor; losing just enough in gambling to assure that the others kept him at the tables while he pieced together what he could from their exchanges.

And that had all taken place in the last week.

Jeremy was exhausted, and no favor in the world was worth pushing himself further.

"Did you hear me, Rook?" Gent pressed from behind him.

Jeremy turned in his chair to face his darker, undoubtedly more handsome colleague, not bothering to hide his feelings on the subject. "I was hoping if I ignored you, you'd go away and take your favor with you."

Gent smiled his usual cheeky grin. Of all the men working in the London League at present, he was the only one who was not at all fazed by the flurry they currently faced. After Cap's house had been invaded by traitors and his family put in danger, they'd all been on higher alert, and their quarry had given them ample opportunity to engage in more activity than they had in months. Operatives, assets, and Shopkeepers, their fearless leaders in high places, were on edge and anxious.

Something was coming, and they all knew it.

Yet Gent smiled, laughed, and looked as if it were only a Tuesday in autumn.

Surely that was a mark of some kind of insanity.

"Not going to work, Rook," Gent quipped, leaning against the door. "The favor is still here, as am I."

"More's the pity," Jeremy muttered, rubbing at his brow. "Come on and tell me, then. I've got loads of work to do."

Gent grunted softly as he entered the room fully, shutting the door. "We all do. It hasn't been this busy in years."

Jeremy looked up at him. "And that doesn't bother you?"

"Bother? No." Gent shrugged easily. "The silence bothers me, and there's been entirely too much of it lately. This is much more my preference. Activity and excitement, progress and anticipation…"

There was some truth to that, and Jeremy could certainly appreciate it. The trouble with their current situation was that there were so many moving pieces that no one had a complete picture.

Well, the Shopkeepers might have, but they weren't sharing.

They never did.

Weaver, for all his apparent fondness for the League, wasn't even letting on, and Jeremy found that significant.

"We'll be onto something soon," Gent said with a sigh, folding his arms. "Something has to give."

"Let's just hope it's not one of us," Jeremy pointed out, giving Gent a knowing look.

Gent nodded once, not needing to elaborate on that point.

Trace's death hung over all their heads, though it had been nearly five years since it occurred. The vacancy created by his demise was the reason Jeremy had been moved from his work at the Foreign Office to the League, and while the purely covert operations was something he rather enjoyed taking part in, that burden had always weighed on him.

Trace happened to leave behind a rather dark and all-encompassing trace, ironically enough.

"Your favor," Jeremy reminded Gent, shaking himself from his gloom. "Work or personal?"

"Would it be entirely unfair to claim both?" Gent grinned briefly.

Jeremy stared at him for a long moment. "Why do I suddenly regret even acknowledging you just now?"

"No idea."

It was astonishing how irritating Gent could be when he wished to, which was odd, as it was usually Jeremy's task to be irritating and unhelpful.

He frowned at his colleague. "Gent…" he said slowly. "What's this about?"

Gent winced slightly. "How well do you know the road to York?"

"There's only one?"

That earned him his usual glare, which Jeremy was far more familiar with.

"Well enough," Jeremy sighed, sitting back in his chair and folding his arms. "Why?"

"I need you to go to York."

3

"Fancy that."

"In disguise."

Jeremy grunted once. "Even better."

"As an escort."

The nod that Jeremy had been in the process of giving paused, and he frowned at his companion.

"As an escort?" he repeated. "Who or what am I escorting? What have you gotten into, Gent?"

"Nothing so very drastic," Gent assured him with a brief wave of his hands. "I just need you to take a carriage to York, and you'll have a driver the entire time, so you don't even have to do that."

"What's inside the carriage?" Jeremy asked, raising a slow brow. "If I'm not driving the carriage, then something must be in it that requires my presence. Prisoners? Traitors? Stolen goods?"

"A woman."

There was nothing complicated about the word, but it took Jeremy a surprisingly long time to process it.

He sat up and drummed his fingers on his desk. "You... need me... to escort a woman to York?"

Gent nodded once, smiling tightly.

"Why?"

"Because her family is in York."

Jeremy glowered at that. "So many questions come to mind."

"Ask them."

"Or you could just tell me exactly what is going on and save us both the length of this conversation." Jeremy offered a placating smile and fluttered his lashes.

Gent made a face and exhaled slowly. "I... *need* you to take my wife's cousin to her brother in York."

Of all the possible women in London that Gent could have suggested, that was the one woman that Jeremy absolutely could not have anything to do with.

Provided Gent's wife only had one cousin.

Jeremy swallowed his protests and the sudden tension in his frame. "Which cousin, might I ask? I'm not too familiar with..."

"Miss Dalton."

Of course it was. Of *course* it was. He'd known it the moment

Gent had said his wife's cousin, but there had been the faint hope that...

Jeremy should have known better than to hope.

Helen Dalton.

No. No, he would not escort her to York. No, he would not ride in a carriage with her. No, he would not stop at inns along the way and take her safety into his hands and be held responsible for everything surrounding her for the time they were together.

No. Absolutely and emphatically no.

He couldn't.

He told himself to say these things. He ordered himself to be defiant, to rise up in indignation, to defend himself. He felt an urge rising within him to laugh in derision.

Yet nothing happened.

Gent offered a sardonic look at his complete lack of response.

Damn.

"Why?" he heard himself ask. Odd, that didn't sound like the refusal he'd been working up in his mind.

"Why what?" Gent asked, his brow furrowing.

Jeremy bit back a groan. "Why does Miss Dalton need an escort to York? Why do you need me to do it? Why aren't you doing it? And what in God's name made you think this was a good time to do it?"

He ought to have been warned off by the very slow rising of Gent's brows, and the tightening of his mouth, but despite being rather observant, Jeremy had never quite managed obedience.

"Because the Season has ended, and she has not seen her brother in some time," Gent recited in a stiff tone, crossing his ankle over a knee. "She wishes to go to York, and as her family has recently left London, she has been under my care. Given that, it is my responsibility to see her safely to York. In case it has escaped your notice, this is not entirely a safe time for anyone with ties to the League, and I cannot have Helen go to York unaccompanied."

That was true, and Jeremy wasn't about to pretend otherwise. If he or his brother had any significant people in their lives, they would have been more watchful and protective, certainly.

But this?

"Add to that," Gent continued conversationally, though his eyes were hard, "that the road to York has had trouble with highwaymen of late, and Margaret is terrified of Helen travelling it alone. Why am I not taking her myself? Because my wife is also terrified of being alone at this time, and she happens to be carrying again, not that it is any of your business, and so a stringent carriage travel ought to be avoided. Will that satisfy you?"

"Easy," Jeremy muttered, rubbing at the back of his neck uncomfortably. "And congratulations," he added with a reluctant smile.

Gent made a soft sound of amusement and ducked his chin. "Much obliged, Rook. I may name it after you."

"Don't do that," he snorted loudly, grinning without reservation. "Poor lad. Besides, Margaret would never let you."

His companion shrugged, still not entirely at ease. "If you do this, she might."

Jeremy shook his head slowly. "That's not a convincing argument, my friend. Why me?"

Gent sat forward, sighing heavily, resting his elbows on his thighs. "Because I need someone I can trust to take Helen to York. That list is growing smaller and smaller by the day with the way our assets and contacts are faring. And… I've been hearing rumors about the road to York."

"What kind of rumors?" Jeremy pressed, sobering at once. If Gent heard rumors of any kind, they were all but proof, and in some cases far better than.

Gent's dark eyes shifted uneasily. "Nothing certain, but the number of highwaymen attacks has increased, yet nothing of real value is taken. Hal visited her aunt last month and her carriage was attacked."

"What?" Jeremy cried, rising from his seat. "Is she all right? Why didn't you…?"

"She's fine," Gent assured him, waving him back down. "You know Hal, she's as hardy as a mule and twice as stubborn. Her only complaint was that her pistol was too difficult to reach with the idiot companion she hired being in the way." He rolled his eyes, shaking his head with a snort. "Trick has been informed and appropriate measures are being taken."

Jeremy sighed softly, still agitated despite the reassurance. Hal was a friend, not just a colleague, and her being alone in London worried him more than he would ever let on. But because her twin was a deep-seated operative, and she herself dabbled in their world as artist, cartographer, and counterfeiter, the danger was more than likely towards those foolish enough to come against her.

More often than not, he forgot that Hal was, in fact, a woman, and the sudden images of her being at the mercy of highwaymen, robbers, or any other nefarious man, set his teeth on edge.

"But it's what Hal said about the attack that worries me," Gent went on, almost musing now.

Jeremy gave him a look. "More than Hal being attacked?"

That earned him a dismissive hand wave. "She can take care of herself as well as any of us. She trained at the Convent, remember."

That was a fair point, but even so…

"What did she say?" Jeremy prodded, sitting back against his chair in thought.

Gent leaned forward, rubbing his hands together. "They weren't paying any attention to her or her companion at all. They nearly tore apart the carriage in search of something, never once asking for money or jewels or anything of the sort. They examined Hal's belongings, thoroughly, but didn't take a single thing. She said they were particularly interested in her sketchbook and portfolios. Almost as if…"

"They knew," Jeremy finished, unease seeping into his stomach and making his skin crawl. "Did they find anything?"

"No, but only because Hal didn't bring anything with her." Gent rubbed his hands together again, lowering his head and shaking it slowly. "If they know about Hal, who's to say that they don't know more? If I go with Helen, even if Margaret allowed it, she could be in more danger. If they know who I am, they'll know she's my wife's cousin. If I travel publicly, they'd know, and they'd attack."

"And you think they wouldn't know me?" Jeremy asked as his mind whirled with the implied ramifications of the situation.

Everything could be much worse than he thought if what Gent was saying were true.

"I don't know," Gent admitted, meeting his eyes once more. "I don't know, Rook. But you're the best alternative. You can assure Helen's safety if her ties to me are compromised, and you can note everything that happens along the road if anything comes."

Jeremy nodded in thought, already analyzing how to situate the carriage and thinking of ways to ensure protection without leaving obvious signs, disguises he could manage, factors to account for when travelling…

He supposed that was his answer then.

"You sound as though you expect us to be attacked," Jeremy murmured, bringing his focus back to his colleague.

He saw Gent's throat work on a swallow. "I do. I don't know why, but I do. It shouldn't happen, she's just a young lady from London. But I'd feel more at ease with you there. I can't ask anyone else to stay with her. Perhaps you're too new to the League to be a target."

Jeremy gave him a look. He'd been with the League for three years, and that was plenty of time to cause enough trouble.

More than Gent knew.

"So why not come up with a legitimate reason to have Miss Dalton stay?" Jeremy asked, offering one last attempt to get away from this insane venture.

Gent snorted once. "Have you ever tried to persuade Miss Dalton to do anything?" He laughed; no doubt certain Jeremy had never done anything of the kind.

For a man who knew so much about so many at any given time and had resources to uncover remarkable amounts of information, he was surprisingly ignorant.

Jeremy had, in fact, tried to persuade Miss Dalton a time or two. He knew just how impossible it was.

Which was why this idea was so terrible.

"So," Gent went on, smiling still, "I have chosen you. And you will be followed by some of my contacts, should trouble arise, and the driver will be one of Skips's men."

Jeremy shook his head slowly. "You are the most overprotective man I have ever met."

"Why do you think I've been saving all of London the last few years?" Gent laughed again. "I can't help myself."

8

"You should see a physician for that."

"But this is my wife's cousin. Her favorite cousin." Gent's look turned rather frank; his meaning clear. "And you know how I feel about my wife."

Jeremy shrugged a shoulder. "But not her cousin."

It was as if Gent sighed without actually sighing. "I'm very fond of her."

"So, send a recruit."

"I'm asking you."

Jeremy gave him a sardonic look. "Asking? Not ordering?"

"No."

Jeremy stared at his colleague and friend, his conscience gnawing at him.

That was it, then.

"Damn you," he muttered after a long moment.

Gent grinned and reached out a hand. "Thank you, Rook. I'll see to all the arrangements. You won't have to worry about a thing."

Jeremy shook his hand hard. "Says the man who thinks I'm about to be attacked by the entire French Faction because his wife's cousin is so enviable a prospect."

"They'd have a time of it if they tried anything with Helen," Gent retorted, his eyes dancing mischievously. "You'll see."

"You owe me!" Jeremy called as Gent left the room.

"I know!"

Jeremy let his bantering mood fall away quickly, and he covered his face with a muffled curse. This was not going to go well at all, and he wasn't sure he had done the right thing by accepting. There was too much at stake, too much to do, and he was too vulnerable to Helen Dalton to have this be anything less than a disaster.

He pulled a piece of foolscap out of his desk and scribbled a quick note. As quickly as he could, he moved to the back door of the building and whistled once. A lanky young man approached, his expression permanently scowling.

"Weaver," he told him, handing the note to him. "Urgently."

The dour look he received amused him. As if these notes were ever anything less. The lad was off without another word, and Jeremy returned to his desk, attempting to get something done amidst the distraction now warring within him.

It wasn't long before the back door was opened, and Jeremy looked up to see a tall man with dark hair, dressed in surprisingly simple clothing, enter his office and shut the door behind him.

"Rook," his guest greeted with a nod.

Jeremy returned the nod. "Weaver."

Weaver sat in the chair across the desk, surveying Jeremy with gravity. "So. A complication."

Jeremy nodded again. "Gent wants me to take Miss Dalton to York."

"Poor you."

The dry response made Jeremy's mouth curve. "Yes, most unfortunate for me." He sobered, his brow furrowing. "Weaver, there's too much to do here for me to leave, and I'm only getting more and more burdened. I can't ask the others to help, nor let them in on *this*," he gestured vaguely toward the papers on his desk. "There's nothing I can do to lessen the burden."

"You're the only one who can do *this*, Rook," Weaver nodded at the papers, his rich voice containing no hint of amusement. "You know that, or I wouldn't have asked it."

Jeremy released a rough sigh. "Why aren't we telling the others?"

Weaver straightened a little. "Because if they knew we suspected something here, they wouldn't be able to focus on anything else. There is a brotherhood in the League, Rook, as you are becoming aware. They've never forgiven themselves. And they have been over everything too often."

"They can't see the forest for the trees," Jeremy murmured.

"Exactly," Weaver told him, folding his arms over his chest. "You have what you need, and the progress you have made already is…"

"Not enough," Jeremy interrupted, jerking his head side to side. "Not enough, Weaver. Not with this, not what we're up against. And now to have to traipse off to York with…" He shook his head again. "What do I do?"

Weaver watched him for a long moment, his mouth twitching at the edges.

Jeremy knew his mentor well enough to know that this was his tell for amusement. He didn't see anything in the situation to possibly to be amused about, but he wouldn't bother pointing that out.

"Go to York," Weaver told him at last. "Getting out of London might be the best thing for you."

Jeremy nodded, disappointed that Weaver hadn't ordered him to remain, but he'd rather suspected it would go this way.

"When you've delivered your precious cargo," Weaver continued, smiling in earnest now, "feel free to stop over in Cheshire."

"Because they are so conveniently located near each other," Jeremy muttered drily.

Weaver hummed an almost laugh. "You'll find the ride rejuvenating, I am sure, after being confined in a carriage with Helen Dalton for so long."

That was probably true.

"Anything in particular I need to see to in Cheshire?" Jeremy inquired, sighing in resignation.

Weaver nodded slowly, his smile turning rather knowing. "The holdings. Parkerton Lodge has been gone over dozens of times, but not by you. The grounds, the neighboring estates, the village... Anything you can think of. I'm giving you free reign, Rook. Look at it from a new angle and find something."

Jeremy swallowed at the severity and significance of his task. "And if I don't?"

"Then we truly may never know what Trace was into, or if there is any chance that he is alive."

Chapter Two

$\mathcal{S}$he had entirely too many possessions, and there was no way she could take them all with her to York.

How had she managed to bring this much to her cousin's home in the first place?

Helen groaned as she waged battle against her trunk again. She *would* get this thing to close securely. She would.

It wasn't her fault that her parents had given up on the Season before she had. Or that she'd had no suitors for the third Season in a row. Or that her three brothers had all managed to reproduce with their wives within the last year, giving her parents additional grandchildren to dote upon.

Their leaving early had nothing to do with her at all. It was purely for the grandchildren.

At least, that was what Helen told herself almost daily in the weeks following her family's departure. Her parents had packed up both of her younger sisters, neither of whom had suitors to speak of, and neither of whom cared.

If it hadn't been for Rafe and Margaret offering her a place in their home, she would have gone mad touring the country from estate to estate with her parents. Staying with the Marlowes allowed her increased status for Society as well as the opportunity to play with and spoil her adorable namesake and goddaughter little Helena Thornton.

She'd had her reasons for remaining in London for the entire Season despite having no suitors and being tired of balls, the theater, and parties.

Well, one reason.

Her departure now was a bitter reminder of the stupid reason it had been.

"Lord, Helen, you have a lot of luggage."

Helen cracked a wry grin at the mocking quip, knowing the phrasing had been specifically designed to echo her usual words. She turned to see her great friend Rosalind Arden in the doorway of her bedroom. "I have a great many gowns, Rosalind. How else could I expect to retain my enviable position in Society?"

Rosalind grinned, her dark eyes sparkling with their usual mischief, nearly the same rich shade as her luxurious hair. She was dressed rather simply today, but the dusty purple color suited her perfectly, as did everything Rosalind ever wore.

It was a trial of rather monumental proportions being friends with someone so stunning.

"Position," Rosalind repeated, her full lips curving. "Is that what we're calling it now?"

Helen laughed and waved Rosalind into the room, sitting on the bed while Rosalind headed for the chair by her toilette.

Yet she did not sit.

Rosalind's fingers traced along the dark wood of the chair, following the engraved patterns absently, while her eyes took on a faraway look.

Helen watched and waited, curious by the change. Rosalind wasn't a fanciful woman, prone to daydreams or imagination, nor did she hesitate when her mind was made up on something. Despite having a set jaw and a clear expression, Rosalind was in every respect reluctant and uncomfortable.

"Rosalind," Helen eventually prodded, setting her hands behind her on the mattress and leaning back on them. "Tell me whatever it is you don't wish to, as I suspect that is why you've come here."

Rosalind's dark eyes flicked over to her, and she smiled just a little. "I'm getting married, Helen."

That was the absolute last thing that Helen had ever expected Rosalind Arden to tell her. Not that Rosalind would never marry, but that it should be announced without any prior courtship.

"To whom?" Helen asked, swallowing the burning in her throat.

13

Rosalind's smile turned wry. "Will Riverton."

"Captain Riverton proposed?" Helen gasped, grinning broadly now. The captain had been pursuing Rosalind on and off for a few years, and Rosalind had never encouraged him in any way. They fought and bantered like unruly siblings, or a couple already wed, and spent such a time in each other's company doing so that Helen had suspected their mutual affection and attraction for quite some time. But Rosalind had been so staunchly adamant that there was nothing between them, despite her attention being on Will far more often than not, and so Helen had let the matter fall to the wayside.

Will Riverton was the catch of the century, and his eye had been on Rosalind Arden from the start.

And now she had him.

"He did," Rosalind admitted with a blush, her smile a most perfect accessory.

"Has he proposed before?" Helen asked without shame.

Rosalind only shrugged. "He might have."

"But you consented this time?"

Her friend nodded. "I did."

Helen laughed breathlessly. "Why? What happened?"

"He's leaving," Rosalind told her with a sigh. "He waited too long to resign his commission, and now he's being sent to the Indies. He can't say how long, he doesn't know."

Helen moaned sadly. "Oh, Roz…"

Rosalind shook her head, holding up a hand. "So, he came to me last night and asked me to marry him. Now. Before he leaves." She smiled tenderly. "He wants me to go with him. He told me he doesn't think he could bear to be gone for so long without me."

The sweetness of the thought made Helen's heart ache, pangs of romantic appreciation and jealousy bouncing around in the pit of her stomach.

"It wasn't until that moment," Rosalind went on, her smile trembling, as her eyes grew moist, "when I had the prospect of him being gone, that I realized how much he meant to me. I had to say yes, Helen. The word was on my lips before I drew a single breath."

Helen stared at her friend, feeling more tossed about than she ever had, and completely beyond words.

Rosalind straightened slightly. "You disapprove?"

"Of course not," Helen retorted with a snort. "I knew he was for you the first time you waltzed together, and that was years ago. I just didn't expect you to change your mind so suddenly."

"I don't understand it myself, but…" Rosalind broke off for a watery laugh. "Helen, I love him. More than I ever expected I'd love anyone. He is the better part of me, and I can't imagine my life without him."

Helen sniffed loudly, finding herself near to tears. "Don't make me cry, Rosalind, I look dreadful when I do."

Rosalind giggled and wiped at the corner of her eyes. "I'm sorry! You should have seen me throughout all of this. Even Will cried a little."

"I'll bet he did," Helen chortled. "The poor man's been in love with you for ages, he'd all but given up hope! When will you wed?"

"Friday," Rosalind replied, turning serious once more. "Lord Riverton procured a special license for us. We are to be married, have a luncheon with our families, and then we are off early Saturday."

"A special license?" Helen repeated suggestively. "Well, well, Rosalind Arden, soon to be Riverton, aren't you a scandalous bride?"

"A dreadfully anxious one, at least," she retorted, grinning without shame.

Helen flopped back on her bed with a groan. "I won't even be here on Friday! How can you get married without me?"

Rosalind whimpered a little. "I know. That's why I had to come tell you straight away. It's not even a real wedding, if that is any consolation at all. Lady Riverton is so distressed by it, as she cannot properly celebrate our union as she did for Sheffield and Sophie. We've promised she can do whatever she likes when we return. You have to be there; you have to help her."

"Too right!" Helen pushed herself up to her elbows and skewered Rosalind with a look. "I'll see to it that Lady Riverton goes above and beyond any celebration to date for the pair of you, particularly as I have had a very great interest in your secret romance for some time now."

"You have not!" Rosalind protested. "How could you know? I didn't even know."

Helen sputtered in derision. "That's because you are blind and stubborn, Rosalind Arden. Ask my cousin, I've been predicting this for ages."

"I will!" Rosalind assured her, turning from the room. "I'm going now."

Only when the room was vacant again but for her did Helen allow herself to fully sigh, sliding back to lay on her bed, staring up at the embroidered canopy.

That was it, then. Margaret was married and a mother, with another child on the way. Rosalind was to be married by the end of the week and spend an undetermined length of time abroad with her dashing husband.

Helen would go to York to visit Charles, the least irritating of her brothers, and strive to not be bored to death or plagued with questions from unfeeling family members who thought that she, as the "pretty one" in the family, ought to have done better.

She had other friends, to be sure, but none that were so close as Margaret and Rosalind. Next Season, she would have to find other near-spinsters to associate with, as she could hardly call herself anything else these days, and the number of those qualifying women that she could tolerate was small indeed. She would have to lower her expectations and standards if she wanted to accomplish anything a young woman of means was supposed to.

But she hadn't the heart for it.

She had done everything right. She'd had the proper education and training, as her governesses would all attest to. She'd had a fair few, and if her brothers hadn't scared most of them away with their antics, there might have been some consistency in her instruction. She'd made the best of it, however, and each new governess had said as much when they'd met her. She was very accomplished, everybody knew that, and she was tolerably attractive, whatever that meant. She flirted with skill and without airs, she was neither particularly encouraging nor overly discouraging, and she always danced when asked unless she had an infallible reason not to.

Yet here she was. Lying on a bed in her cousin's home, waiting to depart for her brother's faraway estate because she had nowhere else to go and nothing else to do.

16

Rosalind was marrying Captain Riverton after years of spiteful bickering instead of proper courtship and flirtation.

Helen had been studiously and pointedly flirting with one man from across and within dozens of ballrooms, music rooms, and theater boxes for an entire year or more and receiving some of the most skilled flirtation in return, and she had absolutely nothing to show for it.

Damn Mr. Pratt and all his fine strutting about.

The man was perfectly ideal in every respect, with his fine fortune and finer clothes, his proper manners and not as proper commentary on everyone and everything, and his sharp wit that never failed to delight her. His eyes were the perfect blend of green and brown, though most everybody in the world would call them simply green.

She knew better. She had seen the hints of brown, the mixture that swirled about with the same intensity that his persona emanated.

Mr. Pratt played a curious game with the whole of London, and she was helplessly fascinated by it. He was absolutely a fop, but without any of the fussiness that usually accompanied that. On the contrary, he was active, vibrant, and exciting. Captivating in his actions and bewildering in his nature, and she had never seen a hint of boredom in his eyes. He knew exactly what he was doing at any given moment, calculating and precise.

Which begged the question. Why?

And who was he under all the pretense?

Helen was fairly sure she knew, having observed him all this time, flirted with him, danced with him, imagined all sorts of in-depth conversations with him... But Mr. Pratt, for all his virtues, had one great and glaring flaw.

He was never consistent.

He hadn't spoken to her in six weeks at least, and what conversation he had engaged in shortly before that shocking length of time had been in the foppish, silly tone he saved for grand public displays. Gone was the spark of light in his eyes she always had seen when they were together. Gone was the mystery of his playing a part for the world.

Gone was her hope for anything at all where he was concerned.

And once the Season had ended, there was nothing else for her to do except go to Charles' home and wait for her parents and younger sisters to arrive.

Then, all of the unsuitable Dalton sisters could be reunited in their mutually unattached states and commiserate on that fact.

Joy of joys.

Helen shook her head and sat up slowly, frowning at her own pathetic indulgences. Imagine hinging all of her interests and attentions on one person, and a man at that. She'd never been that ridiculous in her life, even in her very first Season. She ought to have known better, and certainly had better things to do with her time and energies.

She needed to leave London for some weeks, if not the entire autumn and winter, so that she might properly collect and comport herself in preparation for next Season.

It was entirely possible that she would end that Season as she was ending this one; that is, without a husband or any ties that could lead to one. But she would undoubtedly be in better spirits and enjoy the activity of the Season more completely for not being filled with girlish sensibilities and romantic nonsense.

Rosalind Arden could have a whirlwind marriage and exotic love story to a dashing sea captain who was obsessed with her, that was all well and good. Margaret Easton, now Lady Marlowe, could be engaged in a passionate and thrilling marriage to a peer who was surprisingly dull to everybody not paying attention, that was also agreeable.

Helen Dalton would be the most sensible of the lot and turn over a new leaf. She would let go of her sharp tongue and coy nature, transforming herself into the perfect English miss. Her gowns were already the height of fashion, her figure was as pristine as it had been at seventeen, and her fair hair and complexion had been praised repeatedly as flawless, so all that could remain was her person.

Surely a transformation there would not be too difficult to manage.

She nodded to herself and pushed up from the bed, returning her attention to the trunks scattered about the room.

"I will master you," she muttered at the one she had been

fighting with previously.

For the next several minutes, she waged war against it, and when she had finally proven herself the victor, she left the room, needing to be diverted in some way.

"Helen?"

She turned at the bottom of the stairs to see Rafe, Margaret's mysterious husband, coming towards her, a gentle smile on his face.

As was usually the case, Helen returned his smile without meaning to.

Rafe just had that effect on people.

Well, on the people who didn't think he was the most boring person in all of England. He played a part, too, and somehow managed to convince absolutely everyone that he was nothing, nobody, and quite forgettable. Once someone got to know Rafe, he was anything but forgettable.

Considering Helen first met Rafe during an attempted robbery at her aunt and uncle's home, wherein he had thrashed the intruder to the point of unconsciousness and then kissed her cousin in a way that would have required excessive fanning had she thought about it long enough, neither she nor he bothered with pretending that he was anything other than what he was.

Whatever that was.

"Rafe, did you hear?" Helen laughed and shook her head. "Rosalind is going to marry Will Riverton."

Rafe's eyes widened, and he grinned broadly. "About damn time, I'd say."

Helen took in her cousin by marriage with far more interest. "Do you know everything, Rafe?"

He shrugged easily, still smiling. "Just about."

She loved when he was shamelessly confident. That was when she caught glimpses of the man Margaret must have known, and Helen almost understood their surprising marriage.

Almost.

Rafe was the handsomest man Helen had ever seen, there was no question there, but somehow that all faded when he was surrounded by anyone else in the splendor of a ballroom, where it should have set him apart. He became as simple and unremarkable as a decorative pillar, to the point that only a few guests in several hundred would even recognize the name Lord Marlowe. Only when he was here at home, stripped of the stiff London atmosphere, did he become this. And Helen was rather grateful to call him family.

"Do you have a moment, Helen?" Rafe asked, pulling Helen from her reverie of him.

She nodded quickly. "Of course." She followed as he gestured towards the study and sat herself without invitation in one of the straight back chairs.

Rafe surprised her by not moving behind the desk but sitting beside her instead. "Are you sure you want to leave tomorrow?" he queried, still wearing the gentle smile from before. "Margaret and I wouldn't mind at all if you passed the winter with us."

Helen shook her head. "No, Rafe, though it is very kind of you. I need to separate from London for a time, and York seems as good a place as any to endure a separation."

He nodded slowly, his eyes taking on a sharp light she did not understand. "Very well then. I've arranged a coach for you."

She hadn't expected that, and her smile evaporated as she looked at him in shock. "Rafe, you didn't need to do that. I could have travelled post, and I was planning on it. Millie and I would have been fine travelling by ourselves."

"Well, far be it from me to underestimate Millie's abilities as a travelling companion," Rafe said with a hint of a droll smile, "but no relation of my beloved wife is going to travel post, no matter who she has with her."

"Aww, Rafe," Helen teased, desperate to hide the real emotion she felt at his words.

The look he gave her told her he wasn't fooled by her attempt, but he just continued on.

"I've also arranged for a man to accompany you."

Helen rolled her eyes and huffed. "Oh, yes, we poor helpless females must have a man to protect us."

He smiled a little. "In a word, yes. Humor an overprotective cousin, will you?"

She frowned at him, though her irritation was minimal at best.

Rafe fluttered his lashes pleadingly. "I've never had a sister, and since marrying Margaret, you're the closest either of us have."

Helen blinked at him, an odd lump in her throat. "Lord, Rafe…" she eventually managed.

He grinned at her quip. "Is that a yes?"

She heaved a dramatic sigh. "Very well, I will allow your masculine escort to accompany us. Please tell me he is handsome, at least."

"Oh, he is," Rafe said with a knowing smirk. "Very handsome. I have it on the good authority of at least twenty-seven females."

Helen nodded sagely. "And his mother isn't one of them?"

"I don't even know his mother."

"What a relief."

They shared a smile, and Helen's faded first.

"What's wrong, Helen?" Rafe asked gently.

She shook her head slowly, swallowing. "I feel as though everything is passing me by, Rafe. Nothing in my life has gone the way I planned or expected. Everyone else has what I want, and I can't manage to attain it for myself."

"It being…?"

"Happiness," she half-whispered. "Security. Love." She laughed softly and raised a brow at him. "Matrimony."

He made a soft sound of amusement. "Was that an equation there? Happiness plus security multiplied by love equals matrimony? Because I can tell you, that's not how it works at all."

"I wouldn't know." She gave him a sad smile.

Rafe covered her hand and squeezed. "If there is anything I have learned about life, Helen, it's that nothing, and I do mean nothing, goes as planned. You'll have your grand moment, your sweeping romance, your epic adventure, or whatever it is you are meant to have. Don't look at everyone else and find yourself lacking." He patted her hand once. "It's called a grand finale for a reason, you know."

Helen restrained a giggle. "Are you trying to tell me fate is saving the best for last?"

He shrugged and released her hand. "Could be." He rose and grinned down at her.

She peered up at him with narrowed eyes. "Do you know something I don't?"

21

Again came the shrug. "Probably."

"You are maddening, you know that, Rafe?" she huffed as she rose, giving him a quick hug and a kiss on his cheek.

"Trust me, I am well aware," he assured her, patting her shoulder.

"He is. I tell him that every single day."

They both turned to see Margaret in the doorway, her dark hair fixed at the nape of her neck, her violet eyes trained on them both with amusement and adoration. Fixed on her hip was a dark-haired, dark-eyed girl who smiled at them both, her four teeth beaming proudly.

"My girls!" Rafe crowed, reaching his hands out for his daughter, who flailed for him with a gleeful squeal. He leaned down and kissed Margaret with the sort of kiss that one generally did not share in the view of others.

Helen peered up at the ceiling with a dramatic sigh.

Her cousin laughed and peered around Rafe at her. "Sorry, Helen!"

"No, no, I'm fine," Helen said, waving a dismissive hand. "I enjoy being awkwardly trapped by an amorous couple."

"In *that* case," Rafe said, turning back to his wife.

"No!" Margaret cried with a laugh, pushing off of him. "Helen and I have so much to do before she leaves tomorrow." She held out a hand for Helen, who came to her quickly, and then pulled her out of the room.

"Lord, Margaret," Helen breathed, staring at her cousin with wide eyes. "With a husband like that, how are you supposed to catch your breath at any given time?"

"I don't," Margaret quipped, linking arms with her. "I focus on making him just as breathless." Her full lips spread into a devious grin. "It's a shocking amount of fun."

Helen groaned and looked up at the ceiling again. "Tell me Rosalind is still here and I can pretend I have you both to myself for a while."

"She is, and you can," Margaret assured her. "How would you like a gossip session over tea and cakes?"

"Perfect."

Chapter Three

❦

Two hours down, an eternity to go.

If it kept up like this, Jeremy ought to be just fine.

He was in full disguise, unrecognizable even by Margaret, who had seemed confused by his presence, no doubt expecting to see the man she knew as Rook accompanying her cousin on this venture. He found that oddly flattering, and he was encouraged by her befuddlement.

Helen hadn't even looked at him twice, which satisfied him, and the sheer amount of luggage she had for her jaunt to York was staggering, which amused him to no end. He hadn't ever considered her to be a woman of excesses, but the proof was before him. If he were in a frame of mind to tease her at all, that would be a main point of attack. He suspected she would have an excellent rebuttal already prepared.

Gent had exchanged a firm nod with him, his eyes conveying the gratitude he could not vocalize, but they had discussed the trip at length in the days leading up to their departure, and Gent could have ridden the course in his sleep, so often had he asked Jeremy to go over it.

He was truly the most overprotective man Jeremy had ever met. And he was a covert operative? It was astonishing he had lived this long, let alone that he managed to function in the field after his marriage.

Jeremy's plan for this first day was simple.

Sleep the entire way.

Helen would never engage a sleeping stranger in conversation, so he would only have to worry when they stopped to change horses. Despite travelling in Lord Marlowe's coach, they would exchange the team of horses at least once a day, if not twice. No need for haste, Gent had said, so they might as well not push the horses to their limits.

Jeremy, however, saw a need for extreme haste, so as to save himself from this uncomfortable situation, despite this being the most comfortable coach he'd ever ridden in.

His hindquarters weren't the issue here.

And, of course, Jeremy would never dream of actually sleeping while escorting someone as important to his colleague as Helen, nor with a road as unsuspectingly treacherous as the one they were embarking upon. But he was a very skilled actor, as was required by one in his profession, and beyond that, he had been pretending to sleep for years before he had ever been approached by the Foreign Office.

Only his brother John was better than him at faux sleeping, and that was only because John was a very sleepy person and it was often difficult to ascertain if he were, in fact, awake at any given time.

Pretending to be asleep certainly had its advantages. He could rest while listening without shame. He could mull over various points in his investigation and indulge in careful, thorough consideration of each in a way he'd never have time for otherwise. He could use his other senses and instincts, notice details his eyes might pass over, and prepare responses for imagined scenarios.

Meditation wasn't something he tended to engage in on a regular basis; he rarely stopped moving long enough to properly consider any thought in depth. But if he could accomplish as much as he suspected he would on this trip purely in the confines of his mind, he would seriously consider scheduling a pause in his hectic days.

He'd probably ignore it, as he did with much of his schedule, but it would be in there.

The trouble with being restricted to the boundaries of his mind was that his mind had a tendency to wander, and instead of focusing on the sparse details he knew of Trace's last investigation, as he should have done, his wandering mind fixated on the very woman he was trying to avoid.

Helen had been an utter vision this morning, the morning sunlight glinting off her barely-concealed golden hair, her green bonnet only adding to the richness of the picture. She'd left the ribbons undone, and for some reason, those loose ribbons dancing in the breeze had caught his attention. Her travelling coat mostly hid her figure and the gown beneath, but the cut of the coat had certainly been flattering enough to draw his gaze. The color in her cheeks had been high, her crystal blue eyes clear and bright, and her teasing voice had lilted in the most attractive manner he had ever heard.

Even now, he had wished it had been for him.

This was why he had to be asleep as long as possible. There was no telling what he would do if she engaged him in any sort of banter. His character ought to have been reticent and brusque, a gruff man without any talents in conversation. Just some hired hand her cousin had employed to accompany her and her companion to York.

Jeremy was a very skilled operative, as several associates, colleagues, and superiors could attest. But this woman had the power to make him forget himself and everything he needed to be.

Time and time again from the moment he'd met her, he'd forgotten to be Mr. Pratt, a charming fop and ridiculous accoutrement to any and all events and had been more Jeremy than he'd been in years. They'd danced on occasion, flirted shamelessly, bantered amongst the conversation surrounding them, and she invigorated him to a level that stunned him.

If he were any other man, he'd have courted her in the fastest courtship ever known in the proper world, married her, and be well on his way to wedded bliss by now.

But he wasn't any other man. He was a spy. A covert operative in service to the Crown. A man with experience in the Foreign Office's most secretive quarters, who put himself in more dangerous circumstances than even his London League cohorts were aware, who was lucky to be alive today, or any day, even if it were to be spent pretending to sleep in a coach.

Helen Dalton was more dangerous to him than any foe he had ever faced, because she alone had the power to completely dismantle him.

That truth terrified him.

His one comfort was that he had been able to distance himself before they had ever shared anything personal or significant with each other. Their relationship was strictly superficial and flirtatious, nothing of substance, and could easily be written off as a passing fling.

It wasn't, and Jeremy knew it well, but he could only hope and pray that Helen was less clever and wise than he thought her, on the off chance that she might see it as such.

Perhaps Rogue had the right idea of things with his recalcitrant ways and reclusive nature. He had almost no attachments in the world but for the League and the Shopkeepers, and his life was undoubtedly less complicated for it.

Or it had been, at any rate, before Amelia had found him.

That was an odd stroke of luck. She'd fallen in love with Rogue, not with his public persona, so he'd been able to be entirely himself the whole time.

Fortunate man.

Poor woman.

Jeremy liked Amelia a great deal, but one had to wonder about her tastes and preferences if she had fallen in love with Rogue as he was. Under her influence, Rogue was better behaved than Jeremy had ever known him to be, though not so changed as to be unrecognizable. He, at least, wasn't as smarmy and lovesick as Gent had been, fairly nauseating them all with his bliss.

And then there was Cap... If anyone should have been an example to Jeremy, it was Cap. He'd lost his great love some years before, and married a near-stranger for the sake of his children. A beautiful, lively, captivating girl that Jeremy would easily have snatched up himself had he not been distracted by another woman who had commandeered his senses.

It didn't take long for Cap to be completely head over heels for his bride, as any sentient man would have done, and Jeremy was pleased to see his superior happy once more.

Weaver had his enchanting wife, and the two of them had fairly taken over Europe with their own charms over the years. If they ever went to war again, Jeremy was convinced that placing Lady Emily Rothchild before the opposing forces would settle everything in the space of a single hour. Naturally, Weaver would have to be beside her, and if he were charming, he could help. If he were his usual impudent self, even at his age, he might complicate matters. His wife could rein him in, though. She usually did.

It was dangerous for Jeremy to be thinking of his associates and their wives, because it led him to thoughts of possibilities, matrimony, and the future, and that did not sit well with him.

He couldn't have a wife.

His life hinged on the ability to be flexible with his mortality and his morality, and having ties binding him to another person, or a place, or a group, would hinder that.

John didn't count, he had his own secret life as Sphinx, the great codebreaker, linguist, and pretentious scholar, which the Shopkeepers found invaluable.

Jeremy got into scraps; John played with letters.

Neither of them could talk about it.

Their parents would have been both proud and perplexed, were they alive to see them both working for the Crown.

At any rate, neither of them bore the complications of significant others, and it was better for them to be free of it.

It was.

He jerked with a grunt as a sharp kick landed on his shins, hitting him in just the right way to be acutely painful.

He bit down on his lip, his breath coming in quick bursts through his nose.

"I am so sorry!" Helen gasped, and his eyes went to her involuntarily.

Her eyes were wide, and she appeared truly horrified, her cheeks coloring. One delicate lace glove covered her mouth, and she was barely breathing.

Jeremy stared at her for a long moment, the swaying of the carriage the only movement he allowed himself to make.

"I was trying to shift to find more comfort," she explained in a rush, adjusting herself even now. "For... obvious reasons..."

He could hardly blame her, as her somewhat rotund companion was taking up a deal of space on their side. The woman was kindly featured, though at the moment she was far more asleep than Jeremy had pretended, her mouth gaping open wide and exhaling snores.

"And I lost my footing," Helen went on, now wringing her fingers together. "My boot just shot out and whacked you directly on the shins. I am ever so sorry, sir. That must be painful."

"I've had worse," Jeremy grunted, shifting his voice to a deep growl, keeping his accent thick and common.

Helen smiled kindly, and he blinked at its warmth. "I don't doubt it, if you're an associate of Marlowe. Lord knows what that man is up to at any given time."

He wasn't entirely certain how to answer that. It was a truer statement than she knew, but he could hardly let that on. But he was acting the part of a hired hand, so there was a chance that it could have been accurate, if that had been his position.

So, he did what any good employee would do when put in this position.

He nodded. Just once.

Not that it was a yes or no question, but it seemed appropriate.

Helen's lips curved. "We weren't properly introduced earlier. Or if we were, I don't recollect it."

They hadn't been, which had been a point Jeremy hadn't found necessary to correct.

"I'm Helen Dalton," she went on, still smiling in that peculiar fashion. "Cousin to Lady Marlowe."

Jeremy tilted his head at her, keeping his expression as disgruntled as his character. "Perry," he told her.

Helen hummed once. "Is that your first name or last name?"

"Last."

"And your first name?" she pressed, those eyes of hers warming with the teasing light he adored.

"John."

Her lips quirked wide for a moment, then faded back into hiding. "You don't speak much, do you Mr. Perry?"

Jeremy shook his head, still staring at her pointedly.

She seemed to be considering him with equal interest. "Are you upset with me for disrupting your sleep, Mr. Perry? Or is this how you always are?"

He cleared his throat and shifted in his seat. "Not upset."

"Oh, good." Helen folded her hands in her lap, lowering her chin just a little. "You stare very frankly, Mr. Perry. I hope you are aware of that."

Had he been staring?

Dammit.

"Sorry," he muttered, shifting his gaze away.

"No, no, feel free. Stare all you want. We'll be in this coach for quite some time, you might as well stare now." She laughed a little and he heard her skirts rustle. "No one else stares at me, so I'm quite enjoying myself."

No one stared at her? That was the most ridiculous thing she'd ever said in his presence, and he had to bite his tongue to avoid telling her so. If she only knew how people stared no matter what she did or where she went, the envious glances cast in her direction, or the furtive looks he'd seen many a gentleman send her way.

It was maddening to be the sort of man to notice absolutely everything, and remember it, when he had a personal interest.

"Come now, Mr. Perry," Helen said, her voice teasing again. "I didn't mean to make you uncomfortable. Let us be friends."

Friends.

If she only knew.

Reluctantly, he returned his attention to her and tried to look less surly, though his prosthetic nose wouldn't allow for much by way of real expression. And his wig itched constantly, so he was destined to be cantankerous as a result of being unable to scratch.

Helen's smile was wry now, her eyes practically dancing. "I will let you sleep if you wish to sleep, Mr. Perry. But if you've had your rest, perhaps you will keep me company a while."

Keep her company? That was a terrible idea.

"I've never been much of a conversationalist," he heard himself say, pleased that his speech stayed in character, even if his response was involuntary.

Helen chuckled. "Gracious, Mr. Perry. That was a great many words from you, I'm rather impressed."

Jeremy grunted once. "Don't be."

She grinned without reservation. "I like you, Perry. Sharp-tongued and irritable. My favorite sort."

Great. There went that plan.

Jeremy sat back with a sigh and fixed his gaze on a much safer spot.

The roof.

If Mr. Perry were truly a hired hand for Rafe, Helen would eat her parasol.

No one stared at her like that.

No one.

But if Rafe had brought him on, she had nothing to fear.

Which meant she just had to figure out who he really was, or what his story was, and get the real explanation for his accompanying her. She'd taken many trips across England without an official escort, and no one had even blinked at it. Yet now that she was headed off to York, a trip she had taken plenty of times, she had to have someone with her.

Preposterous.

Still, Mr. Perry wasn't a bad sort. He seemed fit enough, though a bit larger than she had anticipated, and his dark hair and surly looks were off-putting. He'd kept his cap low over his eyes, and only now was it pushed back. She took a moment to really look at him.

High forehead. Tanned complexion. Thick brows. Bright green eyes. Remarkably unshaven for a polite escort.

There were lines at the corners of his eyes and permanently etched into his brow, but he seemed too young for them. She wasn't sure why, but she was certain he was.

And she was just as certain there was something familiar about him.

She'd never seen this man, as he was, but she strongly suspected that the man before her was a fabrication.

The nose alone told her that.

Oh, it was fair enough for a character in passing, or a short interaction, but if one stared at it too long, it took on a life of its own. It was all wrong for his face and natural features, and unless God were truly unkind with his makeup, it was false.

Why would her escort be in disguise?

She had so many questions, and no idea how to go about answering them.

So, she was reduced to keeping Mr. Perry talking until something revealed itself to her; either his identity or a plan.

Fortunately for her, she had never wanted for conversation.

"What about dancing, Mr. Perry?" she asked politely, though she doubted very much that he had actually seen the inside of a ballroom. "Do you dance?"

He seemed to laugh at that, though it was a mixture of a bark and a growl. "Only if I've had too much to drink."

Helen tsked softly. "Do you over-imbibe, Mr. Perry? For shame..."

He clearly heard her teasing tone, and his surprisingly pleasant lips curved crookedly. "Only when I have reason to."

His voice hadn't been so rough just then, and there was a familiar tinge to it that rang in her ears a little.

It was going to drive her mad trying to figure this out, but she had several days and more than enough opportunity, if they sat like this for the whole of them.

"I wish I could drink when I had reason to," Helen mused, pretending at moody indulgence for a moment. "I'm fairly certain I'd be a raving drunkard twice a week."

Now he chuckled and folded his arms across his chest. "Then you are more troubled than you appear."

She smirked at that. "A young lady cannot appear troubled at any given time, Mr. Perry. We must be perfectly pleasant and perfectly poised at all times."

"You seem pleasant and poised enough, Miss Dalton."

Helen forgot all about her investigation as she stared at Mr. Perry, whose green eyes stared at her just as frankly as before. He hadn't said it with any sort of flirtation or flattery, and barely any warmth, but there was something...

"Was that a compliment, Mr. Perry?" she asked, smiling in earnest. "Did you just compliment me?"

He shook his head, pursing his lips in denial. " 'Course not."

"Truly? Because it sounded as though you were."

"Wasn't."

"Liar."

"If you say so."

"I do say so."

"As you please."

"Compliment me again."

"Doesn't work if you're asking."

"Ask me if I care."

"Do you?"

"No." Helen bit back a smile, wondering if he knew that in bantering with her so rapidly, he was losing his accent, which had been rather good. She hadn't known that had been part of the act, too, but it made perfect sense.

Already, Mr. Perry seemed more at ease, and if she kept at it for a bit longer, he might even smile in earnest.

Then she should have him.

Helen Dalton might not be skilled at a great many things, despite being accomplished, but about one thing she could boast; she never forgot a man's smile when it was cast in her direction.

It happened so infrequently that remembering the span of them wasn't difficult.

But it sounded impressive.

"You're unusual, aren't you, Miss Dalton?" Mr. Perry asked, his words sounding more like flattery than the actual compliment had.

Helen nodded primly. "Too right, Mr. Perry. I'm the very definition, you'll find."

He shook his head, almost smiling.

Almost.

"By the end of this trip, Mr. Perry," she went on, excitement rising within her, "you'll see that for yourself."

"I'm sure I will, Miss Dalton."

She was almost there. Almost. Her legs shifted anxiously beneath her skirts and she turned a little more fully towards him. "I mean it, Mr. Perry. I'm utterly bewildering, according to some circles."

"Is that so?" he asked with all the patience in the world.

"It is," she quipped. "I never forget gossip."

"Why do I believe that?"

32

There was absolutely no accent now, and her heart skipped three beats as the rich timbre of his natural voice settled on her.

She knew that voice, if only she could place it.

"Because it's true," she told him, forcing her breathing to calm. "I'm unusual, bewildering, complicated, feisty…"

"Twitchy, too, I think."

His quip drew giggles from her, and she considered him with a greater appreciation. "How's that?"

He shrugged one broad shoulder. "You kicked me."

"I apologized."

"Even so." He rubbed his shin and shook his head. "Twitchy, Miss Dalton. Perhaps not so poised, then."

Helen pressed her tongue to the back of her teeth, fighting a wide grin. His eyes were so alive, so bright, and his giving in and teasing her in return made everything so much better.

For a gruff and irritable man, he was surprisingly vivacious in this regard.

A worthy opponent for her banter.

Someone who clearly loved the volley as she did.

Someone…

"Poised enough, Mr. Perry," she murmured, running her tongue along the back of her teeth in absent thought.

He inclined his head. "If you say so, Miss Dalton."

And then he smiled.

Her breath caught in her chest and she nearly hiccupped at the sensation.

Those eyes. That smile. This banter.

She knew him and knew him well.

"I do say so," she said slowly, straightening up and drumming her fingers in her lap even as her stomach clenched. "…Mr. Pratt."

Chapter Four

$\mathcal{P}$anic set in at once.

"I don't know what you're talking about, Miss Dalton," Jeremy almost stammered. "My name is Perry."

Helen rolled her eyes and scoffed loudly. "And I'm Helen of Troy."

"You could be," he offered, looking her over. "It wouldn't surprise me."

Her look silenced that attempt at flattery.

"Miss Dalton," he said, trying for a placating voice, his mind scrambling. "If I resemble a man you know, it is purely coincidence."

Helen barked a hard laugh. "Coincidence. Mr. Pratt, you're a terrible actor, and your accent has changed no less than three times in the last ten minutes. That alone would raise my suspicions, but you've also gone out of character. The Mr. Perry I accidentally woke was surly and cross, and you are bantering with me as we always do. Please give my intelligence a little credit."

He'd give her intelligence all the credit in the world, except for the jab about his being a terrible actor. He was a very skilled actor, and he knew it well.

He just couldn't seem to remember that when he was around her.

Jeremy scowled at her. "You underestimate your ability to plague a man."

"Enough to forget himself in the midst of his act?" Helen hummed in disbelief. "What a shrew I must be."

"Don't put words in my mouth, Miss Dalton," he told her,

pointing a finger at her. "You're not a shrew."

"I know that," she spat, crossing her arms tightly. "I may be a hoyden, but shrew would be an extreme."

That, at least, was true, though at the moment he thought that line was a bit blurred.

Helen watched him for a long moment, her expression suspicious. "Why the act, Mr. Pratt?"

He opened his mouth, ready to deny it again.

"Don't," she told him quickly, her delicate brow furrowing darkly. "I know who you are, and you know I won't let it go."

Jeremy glowered at her, his emotions wreaking havoc within him. How could he have failed so quickly in this pretense? How could she have seen it so clearly? With all of his years of expertise, he couldn't manage to fool one woman into thinking him nothing but a hired hand?

He'd have to turn in his resignation the moment he finished this task. He was utterly useless.

"I don't have to explain myself to you," he growled, looking out the window at the passing countryside.

"What?" Helen cried in indignation. "I beg to differ!"

"Beg away."

She screeched softly and kicked out her boot, hitting him in the shins again.

"Ouch!" He glared at her sharply. "Don't be a petulant child."

"I'll be whatever I want," she insisted, her eyes flashing. "Especially if you're going to be obstinate and obtuse."

Jeremy rolled his eyes with a groan. "Don't be clever for the sake of a good turn of phrase. I don't care what you think."

Her eyes widened, and her jaw grew tense.

He shifted his legs away, giving her a warning look. "Don't kick me again. I'll kick you back."

"You wouldn't dare…" she breathed.

Jeremy lifted a brow. "Try me."

"Rafe would kill you."

He shrugged one shoulder. "He wouldn't know."

Helen coughed a surprised laugh. "You think I wouldn't tell him?"

"On the contrary," Jeremy drawled, leaning back more fully against the seat, "I am certain you would. And I am just as certain I would have that letter intercepted, and Marlowe would never know what you suffered at my hand. Or foot, as it were."

She sat in silence for a long moment, watching him in shock. "You're not the sort to abuse a woman, Pratt."

He made a sputtering noise. "I never said I would kick you into a pulp, Miss Dalton. One kick in retaliation. You'd be well and whole, barely a bruise to corroborate your story, and one that could easily be explained by a poorly placed table."

Her long lashes blinked once, twice, and then her brow furrowed more. "So, if I kick you, you kick me?"

"Pretty much, yes."

"That's the most ungentlemanly thing you've ever said."

Jeremy let his mouth curve up in a smile. "No, it isn't. It's only the one you've heard. I'm not nearly as much of a gentleman as you've been led to believe."

Helen sniffed once. "You're the one who led me there."

"I know. And a merry leading it was, too."

He was being sharp and scathing and he knew it, but how else was he supposed to maintain any sort of composure here? If he wanted to get Helen safely to York without incident, particularly involving his own sanity, he needed to erect as many barriers as he could.

Keeping her spiteful would ensure a stony silence at some point, and he could get back to processing his investigation on the long road ahead of them.

"Are you telling me," Helen roared, yanking off her bonnet, "that you've been pretending all this time? You've been parading around London, making us all believe you were a charming man with taste and refinement, and instead you're... this?" She gestured at him wildly. "You've been lying the entire time?"

Helen in high dudgeon was a glorious sight, and he took a brief moment to appreciate that fact.

"Oh, don't go casting aspersions you can't prove," he told her, snorting softly. "I don't have to tell you anything about who I am, what I am, or what truth there was in anything I've said or done."

36

"You most certainly do!" she retorted. "You're under contract to my family."

Jeremy threw his head back with a loud laugh. "Under contract? My dear Miss Dalton, I am no such thing. Your cousin doesn't have any power over me, not for this venture or anything else. And even if that were the case, I'd be indebted to Marlowe, not to you. Him, I would answer. You, absolutely not."

Her breath passed through her nose in loud, agitated bursts, and her chest heaved with the force of it.

"You just settle in for the rest of this trip, Miss Dalton," Jeremy told her, his tone turning patronizing. "You won't wish to tire yourself out with such towering fury when it is of no concern to you."

"No concern," she repeated, her voice tight and strained. "No concern."

It occurred to him to tread carefully, but he ignored the idea. "Yes, Miss Dalton. No concern at all."

"No concern?" she said again, her voice rising once more. "My cousin hired a man to see me safely to York, and not only is that man not who he pretended to be, but he's supposedly a gentleman of high standing. And one that I know!"

"Supposedly?" he responded mildly.

"It very much concerns me!" Helen overrode, completely ignoring his interjection. "I am the person being escorted! It's my person you are tasked with protecting!"

"And so I shall, should the need arise." He made a face to indicate his rather nonchalant feelings on that score.

Helen shook her head quickly, her eyes widening. "I wouldn't trust you to protect a bread pudding from a dog, nor do I think you capable of physically competing with the dog in question."

That nettled him neatly, and he frowned at her. "Now wait one minute…"

"Protection." Helen laughed in derision, her hands flailing slightly. "The idea of you protecting anyone or anything is perfectly laughable. I'd be better served having a dock worker escorting me."

She obviously had no idea what sort of men worked on the docks, and the fact that he knew all too well provided several mental images he could have done without.

"Miss Dalton…" he growled.

She wasn't listening to him and covered her face as she laughed further. "Literally, any man from the docks would be better than this. I'd only have to worry about my virtue in that circumstance, and that's even assuming the man would be interested in it."

Jeremy's throat seemed to clench at that, and he fought to find the ability to swallow. "See here…"

"I should have insisted on Rafe," Helen went on, lowering her hands a little, her eyes distant. "Margaret doesn't have to be so possessive of him, he'd only be gone a week, perhaps less. She's grown so emotional since her wedding, so dependent upon him and his presence… Surely his duty lies with me under the circumstances. Margaret ought to find a backbone and be alone for a moment."

Irritation and resentment curled in his stomach, and he fought the desire to defend Gent and Margaret, to tell Helen just how sensible Margaret was for fearing her husband's departure at a time like this… But he kept his mouth shut and settled for grinding his teeth almost painfully together.

Helen looked at him then, as if just realizing he was there with her. "Does Rafe know it's you and not some hired hand taking me?"

Still grinding his teeth, Jeremy nodded once.

She threw up her hands with a loud scoffing sound. "Idiots! I thought Rafe was far more sensible than that, but no! He hired *you* of all people to take me home. You! Oh, he is in for a lashing of untold proportions when I have a pen and paper at my disposal."

"I am perfectly capable of seeing a stubborn brat to her brother's home," Jeremy assured her bitterly, smiling for effect. "Particularly when she is so headstrong as to do so when her family in London has offered to keep her comfortably at little to no inconvenience." He let his smile spread more bitterly. "Well, perhaps a moderate inconvenience, but what else is family loyalty for?"

Helen's jaw dropped, and she made a distressed sound he'd rather thought more attuned to a dog's response than that of a young lady. "How *dare* you!"

That screech, of all things, jolted her companion from her sleep.

"What?" the lady cried, looking around with wide, bleary eyes. "Did you say something, Miss Dalton?"

Jeremy smiled kindly at her. "Oh, she said a great many things, but none of them worth repeating."

"Don't talk to her," Helen snapped. "Millie is my servant, not yours."

"Indeed." He nodded once. "And both of you are under my care, which means I have authority. So, I will speak as I see fit to whom I see fit and when I see fit, Miss Dalton, and if you take issue with that, I invite you to walk the rest of the way to York. I shall provide you what coin I can so you might not be so inconvenienced as to be without funds."

"I have my own funds!" she insisted. "I don't need anything from you!"

"Except my knife and my strength," he reminded her, "and my presence."

"All of those are questionable!"

"Hmm," Jeremy mused as the coach rolled to a stop. "Well, as we are stopping to change the horses, I invite you to relieve yourself and then either return to the coach or start to walk."

He opened the door of the coach and disembarked, looked up at the sun, then back into the coach directly at Helen. "Start in that direction," he told her, pointing down the road. "And just keep going."

He bowed to her, then moved to the front of the coach where Skips's man, Larkin, was already working on the harnesses.

"All right, there, Mr. Rook?" he asked as Jeremy approached.

To his own surprise, Jeremy was seething. "No, Larkin, I am not. If you're all right with the horses, I'll go see to their exchange. One can only hope Gent already made the arrangements. I'm in no mood to be convincing."

Larkin grinned, his face wrinkling with the effort. "That's when I find I do my best convincing, sir."

Jeremy snorted softly and allowed himself a wry smirk. "Indeed. Pity I'm expected to be polite on this venture."

"Most unfortunate, sir. But you see to it, and I'll get us off as soon as we can."

Jeremy nodded and turned down the road for the mews, grateful for the opportunity to stretch his legs, and could only hope that

Larkin was a more pleasant travelling companion than Helen.

There was no way he was enduring another several hours of her company.

"He wasn't serious, was he, Miss Dalton? We're not walking to York, are we?"

Helen barely restrained the instinct to roll her eyes dramatically. "No, Millie, we are not. And he was not serious. He was only being spiteful."

Millie hurried along beside her, dodging tables and chairs in the taproom. "But why should Mr. Perry be spiteful? I mean Mr. Pratt, of course, not Perry. Pratt. I thought... he was a gentleman."

So did Helen. She'd always thought he was a perfect gentleman.

Well, perhaps not perfect, given the sharpness of their bantering and the wicked gleam in his eye when he was being particularly amusing, but perfect enough.

She'd never have expected this.

Why in the world would Rafe have arranged for her to be escorted to York by a gentleman? That was going to do more harm to her reputation than good.

If Jeremy Pratt was not the gentleman she had supposed him to be, in their more than a year of acquaintance, she didn't know what to expect.

Why would he be spiteful?

"Because I was spiteful first," she admitted softly as they exited the inn. "And he's the sort to give as good as he gets."

Millie frowned and huffed as she bobbed along beside her. "I find that to be quite shameful, Miss Dalton. You're a lady, and he ought to be perfectly accommodating to that."

Helen smiled a little. "Not that much of a lady, Millie. And I doubt Mr. Pratt is perfectly accommodating in anything at all."

"I take great offense to that."

She jerked her head up to look at Mr. Pratt, leaning against the coach, his posture too natural and easy for the man she had known.

40

But undeniably attractive for the man before her.

He'd done away with the nose, she was pleased to see, but the matted dark hair remained. His clothing, which she hadn't taken a proper stock of before, having no interest at all in Mr. Perry, was perfectly common, almost threadbare. The linen shirt was far from pristine, the coat a worn shade of grey, and his billowing greatcoat a deep blue. He wore no waistcoat, but the kerchief around his neck imitated the cravat she had seen him wear, although the red fabric was filthy and carelessly knotted.

The only thing she could see that possibly reminded her of Mr. Pratt, as she had known him, were the fine Hessian boots he wore. Although they, too, had been covered in dust and scuffed, so that from all appearances they might suit him.

Helen suspected those boots cost more than the coach they were riding in, unobtrusive and common though it was.

It would have been a crime had they not fit him so well, encasing his legs perfectly, the dark breeches doing nothing at all to hide the strength and power of him.

Perhaps he could protect her after all.

She swallowed once and forced herself to look into his green eyes, an undoubtedly safer target.

"Really?" Helen remarked, quirking a brow at him. "When, pray tell, are you accommodating?"

He shrugged, making a face. "When it suits me."

"That is the least surprising thing you have ever said."

He grinned, his perfect teeth glinting a bit in the light of day. "Again, you are mistaken."

Helen sniffed once, her chest tightening. "Well, obviously I'm mistaken about a great many things, and a great many people."

His smile vanished and a dark glower appeared. "Yes, it seems you were. Get in, both of you. We've got a long way to go."

Mr. Pratt opened the door and gestured to it faintly before turning to the front of the coach.

Helen considered that in confusion. "Not riding with us?"

He didn't even look at her as he swung up to the driver's seat easily. "No, madam, I much prefer to ride up top at this point. Perhaps even drive."

She snorted at that. "If you can drive a team of four and a loaded coach without running us into the ground, I will be most surprised."

"Well, just tell me which side of the coach you're sitting on, and I'll be sure to crash us to the side opposite." He looked down at her pointedly. "Get in or stay here."

Helen looked at Millie, already situated inside the carriage, and she smirked a little as an errant thought took hold.

If Mr. Pratt thought he could escape her by riding atop or, heaven forbid, driving the coach, he was quite mistaken.

"Mr. Larkin," Helen called up in her most pleasant voice.

"Aye, miss?" Mr. Larkin called back, thumbing back his cap to look at her, his smile hesitant.

She beamed at him. "Surely you have earned a rest as well as the horses. Come and take respite in the coach. I have a desperate need for fresh air."

Before anybody could say anything against it, Helen moved to the footholds and hoisted herself up, waving Mr. Pratt over so she could sit beside him.

"Oh, *hell* no," he protested, staring at her with wide eyes.

Mr. Larkin was wiser and jumped down from the seat with a laugh. "If you insist, miss. You just let me know when you've had enough, sir, and I'll take over."

Pratt scowled at him as he disappeared. "I've already had enough," he muttered to himself. "I'll have *him* hitched up with the horses next, so I can whip his flanks."

"Such a pleasant man," Helen sighed as she sat beside him, folding her hands primly in her lap. "Off we go, then, unless you wish to tarry longer."

He glared at her a moment, then muttered something in a language she did not know, but it did not sound flattering.

"And the same to you, I'm sure," she quipped, indicating he should start to drive.

He flicked the reins, still looking at her steadily.

Helen returned his gaze just as frankly. "Something to say, Mr. Pratt?"

"I believe I've already said it." He exhaled sharply and looked forward at last. "You might as well call me Jeremy. There's no need for everybody to know my real name."

"Trying for anonymity, are we?" Helen quipped, wishing she felt any sort of flattery by his offering up that familiarity to her.

He nodded once, a muscle working in his jaw. "Trying. For both our sakes, Mr. Pratt cannot be taking you to York. Mr. Perry can."

In the midst of all her offended airs, Helen hadn't considered that, and it gave her pause.

Her reputation was the only one she had been thinking about, but he had a reputation to consider, as well. Perhaps he had a reason to protect his identity, disguising himself in some way, and keeping to more reserved behaviors.

"You think anyone will know you out here?" she asked, losing all form of pretense. "Or in York?"

He smiled a rather mirthless smile. "I'm afraid people know me everywhere, Miss Dalton."

"Helen."

Jeremy jerked to look at her, eyes wide. "What?" he asked, his voice low.

Helen smiled a little, not even managing the embarrassment to blush. "My name is Helen."

"I know that," he said, still looking somewhat thunderstruck.

She laughed once. "I know you know that, but I want you to call me Helen."

He didn't smile back. "Why?"

"Why?" she echoed. "Because you told me to call you Jeremy, so it only follows that you call me Helen in return."

"That's not a good reason," he insisted. "I'm protecting my identity. You need not worry about yours."

"Perhaps not," she allowed with a sigh, tilting her face back to feel the sun more. "But I'm a firm believer in equality, and, as you said, you've not been hired to see to my care, so there is no need for the distance of station. If you're Jeremy, I'm Helen, and that is that."

He was silent for a long moment, and she imagined him to be staring at her in disbelief. Then she heard him shift a little, and grunt softly, which she took to be an acceptance of her statement.

Odd how that seemed a rather thrilling victory.

"You can ride up here if you like," he finally said.

"Oh, thank you very much," Helen offered, snorting softly.

"But," he continued, "once we get close to the next coaching station, you go back within, and I am the man tasked with your protection, nothing more. Is that understood?"

Helen sighed for effect and nodded. "Eminently."

"Good."

He said nothing else for a time, and Helen cracked an eye open to look at him.

It was difficult to reconcile the man before her with the man she knew, yet it made an odd amount of sense. The same features, obviously, but settled in a completely different manner. Jeremy was intense and focused, harder than he appeared, and yet more mysterious. Mr. Pratt was carefree and playful, charming without excessive flattery, and the slightest bit ridiculous.

Yet Mr. Pratt was there in Jeremy, she could see it. Perhaps not so finely dressed nor so keen to laugh, but the same mischief dwelt in the eyes. Mr. Pratt teased and bantered, mixing compliments with jabs so fluidly they were indistinguishable from each other.

Jeremy was merely insolent.

And yet…

"I'm sorry, Jeremy."

She was sorry? Sorry for what? She frowned at herself, but realized her mouth had more sense than her head.

"For what?" he asked, looking over at her.

Helen gave him a look. "Kicking you. Screeching at you. Calling you a liar. Take your pick."

Slowly, his mouth curved, and her stomach clenched at the sight. "How many do I get to pick?"

She stared at him, then laughed helplessly. "Lord, Jeremy, I don't know. As many as you like. Whatever I should apologize for, I do."

He chuckled easily, and some of the tension seemed to leave him. "Very well, I accept your apology and offer one of my own. I had my reasons for the deception, as did Marlowe, but I apologize for the sharpness that followed its revelation."

"What reasons?" Helen murmured, wondering at the turn of phrase. "Why not truly hire a man for the purpose, rather than have you take it on?"

Jeremy shook his head slowly. "Marlowe entrusted me with his reasons, and I cannot break his confidence."

She had rather expected that, but it was disappointing to have so little by way of reply. "Why take this on if you are not receiving compensation for it? It's a ridiculous scheme."

"I know," he said with a grin. "I told him so."

"Then why?" she asked, throwing her hands up. "You're a gentleman, Jeremy. This is beneath you."

He met her eyes steadily. "Because he asked me to."

"Asked?" she repeated. "Not ordered? Not insisted? Not demanded?"

Jeremy shook his head once. "Asked. Very politely, in fact."

"And you agreed?"

His eyes became teasing, as did his smirk. "Clearly, or I wouldn't be driving a coach beside you."

"Why, though?"

She had to know, had to understand even a little, why the man who was her chief reason for leaving London would agree to escort her out of it.

His brilliant eyes intensified and robbed her of breath. "I liked his reasons. I found they suited my interests all too well."

One faint exhale managed to find its way from her lungs. "And they were?"

Jeremy suddenly winked, his perfect lips curving to one side. "Private, Miss Dalton. I'll thank you to respect that." He returned his attention to the road and began whistling a tune she recognized as a rather merry quadrille.

Teasing her, was he?

Well, he could drive the coach in comfort for a while.

She could play games, too, and he would not be so comfortable then.

Chapter Five

Be spiteful, be spiteful, be spiteful, be spiteful...

To hell with being spiteful.

He just wanted to be for a while.

And with Helen seated beside him, it was fairly easy to do.

Once the initial irritation of her joining him outside of the coach rather than secluding herself inside of it had worn off, Jeremy found himself almost grateful that she was up there with him.

Almost.

So long as the conversation continued to be light and easy, he would be just fine.

But if they got into anything personal, he would be in very great danger of losing himself.

Out here in the countryside, he needed to be more aware than ever. There weren't distractions like he would have had in London, nor the safety of other people to hide behind, metaphorically speaking. There was nothing out here but the two of them and the unknown danger facing them. Danger the likes of which Helen had no idea, and could not.

He not only had to keep her relatively amused and entertained, but also keep her from knowing the true reasons for him being here or suspecting that anything could happen on this trip but the most straightforward matters.

No word of highwaymen or French operatives, no notion of potential injury or death, no concept of the national implications that their being attacked could have.

It was well that he was no longer worried about maintaining a character on top of everything else. It would have been rather a lot to get on with, considering his companion was one of the most inquisitive, curious, clever women he had ever known.

One of the most valuable skills an operative could have was the ability to be flexible.

And Jeremy was.

Sort of.

"How is it that you know Rafe, anyway?" Helen asked, her voice innocently thoughtful, as was her expression.

Jeremy didn't trust that for a moment.

If there was anything he knew about Helen, it was that she was surprisingly devious.

"We've been acquainted for years now," Jeremy said with all the nonchalance he could muster. As he was usually a fairly nonchalant person, both in his private and public life, it was a good amount.

Helen frowned, her brow puckering. "That cannot be true. I have never seen the two of you interact publicly."

That, at least, was an easy one to write off, and he gave her a sardonic look. "How many men does Marlowe interact with in public?"

She considered that with a frown. "You have a point there."

"I try to have a point when I can manage it."

The look she gave him prompted a smug grin on his end.

Helen sighed and shook her head. "None of this is making any sense, Jeremy."

He felt for her, he truly did, but he wasn't about to let that sympathy grant her the answers she sought. "I'd stop trying to make sense of it, Helen. Just trust that Marlowe and I have an understanding, and he came to me for help."

"But why?" she asked almost passionately. "Why?"

Jeremy shook his head, flicking the reins a little. "Because he knew he couldn't leave Lady Marlowe, and he couldn't have you go alone, and rather than hire someone he didn't know well enough to trust with your care, he came to me."

"You're not exactly the obvious choice," she informed him without concern.

He raised his brows at that. "Am I not?" He looked down at

himself for effect.

She groaned dramatically. "Stop being difficult. You know what I mean."

He laughed once and raised a surrendering hand. "Fine, fine, I'm sorry."

"I doubt that," she muttered. "Just as I doubt that whatever association you have with Rafe is limited to just the two of you."

Jeremy said nothing, his expression carefully blank.

Helen scowled, and huffed in her seat, sending her skirts dancing a little in the breeze.

He was amused by her efforts to pry any information from him. So sweet, so innocent, having no idea what sort of questioning he had undergone in the past to no avail. Why, interrogation had been part of his training for the Crown, and that exercise hadn't been a particularly pleasant experience.

But he'd passed it, and the enemy's attempts had only been worse.

But that was another story for another time.

Not for her to hear, but he might have to tell the League about it. They always liked good stories about suffering and beating the enemy and living to tell about it.

And someone needed to be able to top Rogue.

"What is it you all do, anyway?" Helen muttered moodily. "I know Rafe isn't the boring man he pretends to be, and I know you're not a fop."

"You don't know that," he protested with all the haughtiness Mr. Pratt had ever employed in Society.

Helen rolled her eyes. "You're not *all* fop, then. What do you do, Jeremy?"

There was no point in pretending he was just Mr. Pratt the fop, so he allowed himself to sigh and give her a little bit of the truth.

A very little bit.

"Whatever I'm told," he admitted, shrugging carelessly. "Parade around in Society, race off to save innocents, slum around the Seven Dials…"

"Escort fair maidens to faraway locations to ensure their protection?" she added, the derision ringing clearly in her tone.

Jeremy grinned at her. "I'm especially good at that one."

Helen laughed merrily, clapping her hands together. "You do whatever you're told. You would have made an excellent soldier, I think."

He made a soft noise of amusement. "I *did* make an excellent soldier."

Her gasp caught him somewhere in the vicinity of his stomach. "You were in uniform?"

"For five years," he said with a nod.

It seemed a lifetime ago, but he had been. Before he'd been assigned to the Foreign Office, before he'd become the Rook, he'd been just Lieutenant Pratt, anxious and eager to prove his worth. It had only taken two of those years for his commanding officers to introduce him to Lord Rothchild, who was quick to recruit him for the Foreign Office. Weaver, as he was known, instructed Jeremy to keep his commission, and he had served in the Army as part of his cover those first few years. The tasks had been simpler back then, but he hadn't known it at the time. His inexperienced mind thought it was all the height of intrigue and danger.

Only after he'd resigned his commission and had gone completely covert did he truly understand.

The Rook had been born then, and there had been no looking back.

Helen made an appreciative sound, bringing him back to the present. She made a show of fanning herself. "Oh, to see you then…"

He harrumphed a little. "I'm much handsomer now than I was then. I was a puppy."

"I adore puppies," she told him frankly.

"Men are far better," he assured her, shaking his head.

Helen shook her head in return. "Far more trouble, you mean."

"And far more fun."

"Lord, Jeremy…" she laughed, her eyes widening.

He shrugged again, grinning at her startled expression. "Surely you know that by now, Helen."

She coughed and looked away, her cheeks heating. "I know nothing of the kind. If you paid as much attention as you ought to have done, Jeremy, you would know full well that I'm practically a pariah in Society."

Jeremy scoffed in disbelief. "I pay plenty of attention, and it's not true."

"Then you know more than I do." She looked back at him with a very faint smile. "I'm a spinster."

"Really?" he asked in a flat voice. "Says who?"

Helen's expression turned to confusion. "No one that I know of, but surely that's clear."

He swung his head slowly from side to side. "No, it isn't. And if no one has said you're a spinster, there's no reason for you to think yourself one. I doubt anybody pays that much attention to things like that."

She tossed her head back and laughed, the sight and sound arresting his attention and diverting his train of thought.

By heaven, she was a beautiful creature. Her throat danced with her laughter, her skin glowed with it, and that glorious hair seemed ready to break free from the pins and plaits restraining it. Her laughter was low, as was her voice, and had a raspy, throaty quality that sent his toes tingling.

He needed her to laugh more.

No, less.

More and less.

Less and more?

"What's so amusing?" he managed to ask.

She looked back at him, remnants of her laughter in every feature. "You think people don't pay attention to things like spinsters? Jeremy, that's exactly what people pay attention to. Maybe you aren't a fop after all."

He found himself returning her smile. "Maybe not, but I certainly do a decent impression of one."

Helen hummed a little. "Yes, you do, don't you?" She gave a little giggle, her eyes still trained on him.

Jeremy returned his attention to the horses, exhaling very softly.

Less. Definitely needed her to laugh less.

"How did you meet Rafe?" Helen asked some time later, after they had changed horses again and had traded places with Larkin and Millie.

That had been Helen's insistence, as she'd had enough of the sun, and Millie seemed rather taken with Larkin, so it only made sense that they should ride together.

Larkin had not seemed to mind at all, which made it even better.

Jeremy, who had apparently been close to dozing off, looked up at her suddenly. "How what?"

Poor man, having to endure her endless chattering when he was clearly exhausted.

She gave him a pitying smile. "How did you meet Rafe?"

He cleared his throat and shifted in his seat. "Don't recall, really. Mutual acquaintances introduced us."

She couldn't find anything wrong in that statement, but it was a rather weak explanation. "Did you meet him as Lord Marlowe? Or as the Gent?"

She'd been waiting to reveal that bit of information, but she was fairly certain now that the two were connected somehow.

Jeremy gave almost no reaction to the name, but he did turn very slowly to look at her. "The Gent?" he asked with only mild interest. "I've heard that name before, but I never presumed…"

Helen barely avoided rolling her eyes, "Fine, don't talk about it. Just listen."

He shrugged, which he seemed to do quite a lot, and sat back, folding his hands together and looking rather attentive.

"I met Rafe as the Gent," Helen told him, smiling at the recollection. "He broke into my uncle's house to rescue Margaret and me from a gypsy intruder." She smiled a little. "Though I suspect I was only a very minor thought in that process. Margaret was his chief concern, and who could blame him for that?"

Jeremy said nothing, nor did his expression change.

Maddening man.

"I tried to convince Margaret that we both needed to flee the house for help, but she insisted that help was in the study." She let herself laugh at the irony now. "I had no idea that my cousin had fallen in love with a man of the streets named the Gent, but it became perfectly evident that was the case when I caught them in a passionate embrace when I went to the study myself."

One corner of Jeremy's mouth curved up, but nothing else in his expression changed.

Helen shook her head, more at him than at the story. "He was carted away and taken to Bow Street or the Foreign Office, I can't recall, but Margaret and I were convinced that he was dead or worse."

"What's worse than dead, I wonder?" Jeremy asked quietly.

She ignored him. "But then lo and behold, Margaret was getting married to a man I couldn't recall ever seeing, which was a shame, as he was furiously attractive."

Jeremy snorted once. "Passable at best."

"I don't know how he does it," Helen went on, paying his remark no mind, "but it took me several months into their marriage to realize that the boring and handsome Lord Marlowe was, in fact, the Gent." She smiled a little at the memory of that day. "He wasn't particularly keen that I'd figured that out."

"Then I doubt he'd be pleased to have you tell me," Jeremy pointed out.

She lifted her eyes to him. "That would be true, if you didn't already know."

He raised a dubious brow. "You think I do?"

"I think you do."

"That's your prerogative."

Helen stared at Jeremy for ages, but he only stared right back.

This was getting her absolutely nowhere.

"Is there anything in this world that you can actually tell me, Jeremy Pratt?" she asked with a heavy sigh.

He seemed surprised by that. "Of course there is. You only need to ask the right questions."

Oh, was that all? He made it sound so very simple.

"Is your name really Jeremy Pratt?" she inquired in a monotone.

"Yes."

"Where did you learn to drive a coach?"

"My father taught me."

"Why?"

"So I wouldn't pester the servants when I wanted to take a team out. We didn't have many, so the demand would be felt if I did so."

That was interesting, and she cocked her head at it. "You seem to have a fortune, though."

He nodded sagely. "I do. Not extensive, but enough."

"How?"

"Army, remember? And I have investments, holdings, and the like."

That almost made sense, but no officer she had ever met had gained a fortune from it. But she would never claim to understand investments and holdings, so she supposed she would have to take his word for it.

"Where are you from?" she pressed. "Originally?"

He smirked at that. "Manchester."

"Truly?" She looked him over as if expecting to see traces of Manchester on him. It was the most unexpected place he could have said. "You don't sound like it."

Jeremy laughed once. "I should hope not. John and I worked very hard to rid ourselves of accents."

Frantically, Helen's mind raced to recall if she knew a John with whom he should be tied. "Your brother?" she ventured.

He nodded. "Older brother, yes."

She frowned and leaned forward. "Did I know you have a brother?"

He chuckled again and crossed an ankle over his knee. "I don't know, did you?" He shook his head. "John doesn't go out into Society much. Bit of a recluse, but as good a man as any I've found."

"You're biased," Helen pointed out, smiling at the real fondness she heard in his tone.

"Shouldn't I be?" he shot back. "Isn't that what siblings are for?"

In theory, she supposed so, but that hadn't exactly been the case in her family. "Not for me," she said with real honesty. "I come from a large family, three brothers and two sisters, and while I adore my parents, I am convinced my parents only produced one child of sense."

Jeremy was already nodding before she finished. "The brother we are taking you to, yes?"

Helen coughed a laugh and shot her foot out to whack him in

the shin again.

He retaliated with a much softer kick at hers.

Her eyes widened at the contact, and she somehow grinned at him with her mouth wide open.

"You kick me, I kick you, remember?" he reminded her without shame.

"I thought that was only said in spite!"

He shook his head, smiling easily. "I never make spiteful threats I wouldn't follow through on."

Helen almost commented on that, doubting very much that it was true, but something held her back.

Bantering with Jeremy, though she'd only done it for a few hours, was far more fun than bantering with Mr. Pratt had ever been. She would never have expected that, had she considered that Mr. Pratt wasn't what he had seemed. Jeremy was so much more than Mr. Pratt had been, with more secrets and mystery and action than she'd imagined. Whatever annoyance she had felt earlier in the day about the deception was long gone.

She rather liked this version of the man, and she wasn't about to complain about the chance to know him.

Provided he wasn't lying to her now.

She couldn't believe that, not if she wanted to value her sanity.

She couldn't question every word, every look, every quick-witted response he doled out. She had to believe and trust that he was being truthful, even if it weren't the whole story. She could cope with not knowing everything if she could at least piece together what there was.

She couldn't have said why, but it suddenly seemed particularly important that she get to know everything she could about Jeremy Pratt.

There was a ticklish sort of excitement at the idea.

"Why did you agree to come with me?" she whispered before she could stop herself.

Jeremy's amusement faded, and his eyes fixed on her with the same striking intensity as before. "I told you, Helen. I had my reasons, and I liked Marlowe's reasons. I can't say more than that."

"Why?" she asked again.

She watched his throat work, and he shook his head. "Maybe I like York."

She deflated at the obvious fabrication. "I doubt that very much."

"No, I do," he said, though there was no conviction in his voice. "York Minster is a lovely place."

Helen smiled weakly at that. "True, but I still doubt it."

"Yorkshire is a beautiful county."

She nodded, looking out the window, feeling forlorn. "It is. I thought Charles a bit strange for procuring a house there, but it seems he was wiser than I thought. I love to wander the grounds, so rich and green and rolling…"

"But it is almost autumn."

"All the better. The trees will be turning colors, and Yorkshire will be all the more brilliant for it." She sighed at the prospect. "There's a rather majestic tree at the back corner of the grounds, and its branches are thick and full. I can sit under that tree for hours and never feel the sun fully. I can lay beneath its leaves and catch glimpses of the sun as it moves overhead, each ray turning the leaves more brilliant in their shades… So many daydreams and imaginings can take place there."

"And what do you dream of, Helen?" Jeremy asked, his voice lower than it had been. "What do you imagine?"

You.

The thought caught her off-guard, and her cheeks heated at it. Though it was true, she could hardly say it aloud. The last time she had been at Leighton, she hadn't known Jeremy, but she had imagined romance, certainly, and a dashing man to sweep her away.

At the moment, the man who fit that persona was sitting across from her in the coach. Whether he remained there was still as much a mystery as he himself was.

Helen smiled at him, though she felt the smile shake. "That's private, Jeremy. If you needed to know, you would."

She knew at once that he saw her hesitation and distress, but he played it off by dramatically scoffing and rolling his eyes. "That's so unfair," he retorted. "You can't use my words against me."

"I just did." She raised a brow. "Maddening, isn't it?"

He grumbled under his breath and looked away.

"So, you can drive a coach," she observed, straightening up and forcing her melancholy aside, "you were in the Army, you can mimic accents, you can speak French, you can disguise yourself as either a fop or a working class man, and you can dance like an instructor. Anything else you feel like sharing?"

Jeremy's lips pursed in thought, the motion of the carriage swaying him a little. "I've been known to fight for sport. I happen to have an excellent singing voice, if I do say so myself. And I can spot a liar in less than thirty seconds."

Helen stared at him for a long moment, smiling in spite of herself. "Lord, Jeremy… what can't you do?"

His mouth curved, those perfect lips driving her mad. "Starch shirts. Tie my own cravat. Eat peas with a knife."

She giggled helplessly. "Nobody cares about those things."

Now Jeremy's smile deepened, and with it the swirling feeling in the pit of her stomach. "Then I can do everything, Miss Dalton," he told her, his voice dipping lower still. "Absolutely everything."

Lord, Helen…

She swallowed at the sensations swirling about her. "You are rather sure of yourself, aren't you?"

Jeremy, no doubt having no idea of the effect he was having on her, smirked. "I have to be. No one else is."

There was a hint of raw honesty in his voice, and she nearly swooned at it.

No one else was?

That was simply not true.

"I am," she admitted softly.

Jeremy's eyes widened, and his smile faded slowly. There was no sound but the carriage wheels and the horses' hooves, and the pounding pulse in Helen's ears.

"Well," Jeremy finally said, swallowing once, "I'm afraid I don't have words to respond with."

Somehow, Helen was able to smile at that. "That's a first."

He returned her smile. "Yes. Yes, it is."

Chapter Six

The night at the inn was spent rather quietly, but Helen really hadn't expected anything less. It ought to have been quiet.

What she hadn't expected was her disappointment that it had been quiet.

Not that she had anticipated anything loud or frivolous, but after the exciting day she'd had bantering and bickering with Jeremy, she had rather expected something...

Anything really.

Visions of sitting in the taproom at a worn table before a roaring fire laughing hysterically kept coming to mind, though she was well aware that Jeremy was not one of her female friends inclined to stay up late and chatter endlessly until they were so giddy as to be insensible.

But he was charming and amiable, and mischievous.

Yet he had behaved with all the manners of a perfect gentleman, and even the stodgiest of Society patrons would have agreed.

It was oddly disappointing.

They'd had a hearty dinner at the hands of their hosts, who hadn't been much for conversation, and Jeremy had regaled her with stories from his youth in Manchester.

No one would have believed that Mr. Pratt had been that rambunctious as a lad.

But it seemed to fit rather perfectly with Jeremy.

He'd surprised her after dinner by seeing her to her room and bowing politely at the door before striding off down the hall. Helen had stared after him, stunned and bewildered.

Not that anything untoward should have happened.

But surely *something* should have!

It had taken her hours to fall asleep, so often she tossed and turned over their conversations that day, and before she'd known him as Jeremy, trying in vain to find the glimpses of Jeremy in the foppish Mr. Pratt. She imagined dozens of conversations they would have the next day, quips she would make, snappy retorts she could give, always saying the perfect thing to make him smile in the most charming way.

Surely this was the most ridiculous she had ever behaved in her entire life.

This morning at breakfast, he'd not even been in the taproom, which had disgruntled her, but Mr. Larkin and Millie had been perfectly acceptable companions for the meal. Larkin had surprised her by informing her that the coach was already prepared, and they were ready to depart at her convenience. She'd expected Jeremy to have still been abed, given the relatively early hour, but as they had walked out to the coach, he was there as prepared as any servant to attend his mistress in loading the coach.

Millie accompanied them inside the coach and had almost immediately fallen asleep.

To Helen's dismay, so had Jeremy.

So here she sat, the swaying of the coach lulling everyone but her into slumber. She had never been one for coach sleeping. And given that she had expected another full day of conversation and wit, she had neglected to bring a book in the coach with her. Not that she was a great reader by any stretch, but it would have been some sort of amusement.

All she had now was the passing scenery, and as it was a rather gloomy day, it did not lend itself to much by way of admiration.

What a surprise that her expectations had gotten her into trouble and left her disappointed. It was the perfect theme for her life, though she doubted anyone could be aware of that. She'd always covered her wounds with cynicism and comedy, finding that most people were perfectly willing to be distracted out of their fleeting concern, and most of those people were not intelligent enough to know when they ought to be concerned anyway.

There was no reason for her to have expected anything at all.

Jeremy Pratt was an actor in so many ways, and there was nothing to say that the man she had bantered with yesterday would be the man she rode with today. The man she had flirted with in London was not here, and it was entirely possible that yet another version would present himself to her before too long.

Provided, of course, that whomever he was ever woke up.

Until then, she would just lay her head against the wall and stare forlornly out of the window, cursing herself for dressing in one of her more fetching gowns when it would all be for naught. It was even one of her favorites; white muslin with green and yellow embroidered flowers and a green ribbon in her hair, and instead of the dark travelling coat of yesterday, she'd pulled out a lighter, more flattering yellow pelisse.

It was the most impractical sort of travel ensemble conceivable, but practicality stood no chance against a woman who wished to make an impression.

Idiot female sensibilities.

"You're an idiot, Helen Dalton," she muttered to herself, allowing a plaintive sigh to escape.

"Well, that's a bit harsh, don't you think?"

Helen jerked to look over at Jeremy, who was not so very asleep now, though he still leaned heavily against the wall, his green eyes watching her.

She swallowed once. "Not really. Fairly accurate, actually."

His lips quirked just a little. "I doubt that."

Helen shook her head with determination. "I'm afraid you don't know me well enough to say that, Jeremy."

He frowned suddenly, a deep furrow appearing between his brows, and straightened. "I've known a great many idiots in my life, and I have to say that you don't even remotely resemble any of them."

That made her smile, though she couldn't manage much of one. "I've heard I don't resemble much of anyone. Even my own siblings."

"I thought you looked remarkably like your mother," Jeremy commented in an almost offhand way. "Younger, of course. Less wrinkled, though your mother doesn't have many of those to speak of, and your skin is tighter, particularly about the face."

Helen clamped down on her lips to keep from giggling wildly.

Jeremy pretended not to notice. "Even so, your mother is still a lovely woman in appearance, which bodes well for you in the future, I think. I'm not particularly acquainted with her personally, for which I blame your surprising lack of proper manners…"

A burst of laughter escaped Helen's lips, and she covered her mouth quickly.

"But everything I've heard of your mother seems perfectly proper, so resembling her would be rather fortunate for you." Jeremy shrugged easily, still not commenting on Helen's giggles. "Unless, of course, she happens to be an idiot, in which case you are quite doomed."

Helen fell back against the seat of the coach, not even bothering to restrain her laughter now. The idea of her mother being an idiot was laughable, but it was his utterly perfect description of her that sent her into hysterics.

Jeremy considered her with marked interest. "Well, perhaps *now* you might be an idiot, you look quite done for, and we've still quite a way to go. I doubt Marlowe will be pleased to have you presented to your brother without any faculties, considering you must have left London with them."

"Oh, stop," Helen pleaded, one hand clasped to her chest as if it could stop the tide of laughter. "Stop, I can't…"

"Deuced uncomfortable things, faculties," he commented without concern, shifting in his seat. "I try to do without mine, if I can. Tends to make the day pass with a bit more ease."

Helen looked at him, grinning while she continued to laugh. "I rather like my faculties."

His look turned almost intrigued. "Yes, so do I."

"Jeremy!" she shrieked, shocked and delighted all at once.

He grinned, completely unapologetic. "What? You like them, why can't I?"

Her cheeks heated, and she struggled for an answer, considering she was still full to the brim with giggles. "I hardly think we are talking about the same thing…"

His mouth gaped in shock. "Miss Dalton! Are you accusing me of impropriety?"

"I doubt it would be the first time," Helen muttered, still

smirking at him.

"It most certainly would!" Jeremy protested hotly. "I have never been improper with a woman in my entire life, not in word or thought or deed."

Helen shook her head slowly. "I doubt that very much, but I apologize for offending your honor."

His eyes narrowed, but his mouth curved again. "Apology accepted. And despite your doubts, I do have honor." The smile faded slightly, and his eyes lowered, growing distant. "It might be all I have, come to think of it."

That was surprising, surely there was much more he could claim to possess. He wasn't the sort to be downtrodden about anything, and it seemed wrong to see him anything less than jovial.

Then again, she didn't know him very well, either. How was she to know if he were always cheerful when he was out of the public eye? He might have been pretending just as much as she had, though her moments had, admittedly, been fairly sparse in number.

What if Jeremy was more prone to this than she could have pictured?

Would it tarnish her image of him?

She snorted at that. Image. What image? She didn't have an image that could be trusted where he was concerned.

"And what is so amusing about that?" he demanded.

Helen looked back at him in surprise. "I wasn't aware I had done that aloud."

He sniffed and adjusted his greatcoat. "Well, you did, and I demand to know your reasons for it."

There was no way she could tell him what she was thinking, as it was entirely centered on him and his person, and the truth of who he was. Admitting to thinking of him was a degree of embarrassment she was not willing to endure.

And yet...

"I was just wondering which version of you is real," she asked, keeping her tone innocent and light.

Surely, she could ask that without him thinking anything untoward of her.

Or suspecting.

His eyes widened in surprise. "Pardon?"

Helen shrugged one shoulder, smiling with a hint of apology. "I've known at least two versions of you in the time we have known each other. Three, if you count Mr. Perry. And four, if..."

If she counted the distant man of recent days.

Which she did.

She cleared her throat and raised a teasing brow. "So. Which one is the real Jeremy Pratt?"

He was silent for a moment, staring at her as they both swayed with the motions of the carriage.

His silence worried her. It should not have been a complicated question, and yet he hesitated.

"This one," he said in a surprisingly rough voice. He prodded himself in the shoulder with a finger. "This man here. This is Jeremy Pratt, born in Manchester, younger son, mischief maker and irreverent lout."

Helen smirked at that. "Apparently honorable, capable of a great many things..."

Jeremy returned her smile, though his was gentler than she'd expected it to be. "Coachman, footman, soldier..."

"So many things, Jeremy," Helen commented. "And all of them are you?"

He nodded, his smile turning wry. "Bewildering, right?"

"Very." Her admission was blunt, but she couldn't apologize for it.

Jeremy winced and leaned forward, keeping his gaze fixed on her. "I'm sorry, Helen. I..."

She shook her head quickly, desperate to stop the emotional tide rising within her at his words, the meaning behind them, and anything more than this light interaction.

"Nothing to apologize for, Jeremy, honestly."

He looked as though he didn't believe her, but he was apparently too much of a gentleman to say so.

Helen forced herself to smile with as much deviousness as she could. "How much Mr. Pratt is in you, Jeremy?"

Jeremy was not as easily distracted as the other people Helen fooled with her wit, but he still grinned with an echo of the airs she had seen around the ballrooms of London.

"Just enough, my dear. Just enough."

There was something Helen was not telling him, if not several things.

He shouldn't have been surprised, given that he was hardly an example of openness and sharing.

In his years of training, he had learned to read people carefully, and usually with a fair amount of accuracy. He might not know the details, but Jeremy was certain that Helen was hurting. And he was equally as certain that he was at least partially to blame.

That scared him in a way he had not felt in years.

How had he hurt her? When? Where?

Why?

Why was a terrible question to ask at any given time, but it might have been worse than ever with her tender heart at stake. Why should his actions hurt her? Why should she care?

Just… why?

But gentlemen did not pry, and he was a gentleman.

Sort of.

At the moment, he wished he would be more of that hired hand than a man of birth, and then he could ask whatever questions he wanted. If he were truly in disguise, acting as an operative, he could be whomever he needed to be to get the information he needed. He'd been ruthless in certain circumstances, and in ways he could never share with anyone but his superiors. In most cases, he only needed to be impertinent and persistent.

Unfortunately, this was not one of those times.

Not with Helen. Everything was different with Helen.

Last evening at the inn, he'd kept up a steady stream of entertaining conversation, and then he'd seen her to her room, like he truly had been hired to look after her. But it was the only way that he could continue on with the rest of the evening the way he needed to.

She needed to be safely ensconced in her room while he met with Gent's contacts.

He'd been down with them at least an hour, possibly more; he hadn't really checked the clock. Half of them had followed the coach from a distance, fully out of sight, but close enough should the need arise, and the other half rode ahead of them, ensuring a clear path for them to tread. They took note of anything suspicious in the area and compared notes that evening.

Helen was more protected than the Prime Minister, it seemed.

Overprotective fool, that Gent.

And yet...

Gent hadn't been the one to sleep on the floor outside of Helen's door last night just to make sure she was safe.

That had been Jeremy.

And he'd not slept well. The fear that Helen would be a nighttime wanderer and discover him there weighed heavy on him. It seemed to jerk him from the brink of sleep whenever he got too close. Not that he usually slept well on assignment, but that was a different sort of anxiety. A wariness that thrilled him in a way.

There was nothing thrilling about sleeping on the floor on the threshold of the woman he...

Well, it was ridiculous and rash, and rather uncomfortable.

So, he'd fallen asleep the moment they'd been situated in the carriage, despite wanting to spend as many moments with Helen as he could steal.

And now to see the drawn expression she'd worn when she thought herself unobserved, to hear that she was confused by the variations of himself she had been privy to, to feel ashamed of himself for not being able to remove her concerns, to relieve her anxieties, or to do anything remotely resembling the things he wished...

He was a spy, had seen more of the world than he'd cared to, felt guilt and torment and fear to untold degrees, and yet nothing in his past had prepared him for this.

He watched Helen now, marveling at her beauty in the morning light, loving that she chose not to wear a bonnet today. There was nothing to obstruct his view of her impeccable bone structure, her glorious hair, or those brilliant eyes of hers.

His own eyes drank in the sight of her as if he had never seen her before in his life.

Clearly, he had slept poorly indeed; he had no control of himself.

Helen's brow furrowed a little, her eyes lowered, her mouth turned down, and he wondered at it.

"Why the frown?" he asked, tilting his head. "What's wrong?"

She looked up at him, then smiled in a way that he almost believed. "You weren't supposed to see that."

He smirked, recognizing a proper attempt at defenses when he saw it. "Too bad for you, I did. Let's hear it."

Her mouth tightened. "I don't think so. It's not seemly."

"When has that stopped you?" he queried.

Helen's jaw dropped. "How dare you…"

Jeremy rolled his eyes. "Come on, Helen, you know I didn't mean it that way. You and I both know that you are not a meek little miss who always behaves with exactness. You're bright, vivacious, and bold without being brazen in any way. It's one of the things that drew me to you in the first place."

Her eyes widened, and he could see every single breath she took.

That hadn't exactly been what he'd intended to reveal, but it wasn't something he could take back, and he didn't particularly feel like doing so.

"So," he went on with a slight clearing of his throat, "while your maid here is sound asleep and won't have any idea how unseemly you are being by confiding in a gentleman of quality…"

Helen snorted loudly, surprising him.

He gave her a warning look. "Go on and tell me what makes you frown and furrow so."

She stared at him for a long moment, and he was half convinced she would refuse him, but something told him to hold steady the course, so he continued to stare back.

Finally, Helen heaved a heavy sigh and seemed to wilt before him. "I'm lost, Jeremy."

"Hmm," he mused, looking out of the window. "I'd say we're still in Cambridgeshire somewhere."

A sharp whack across his shins drew a pained laugh, and he quickly tapped his boot against hers, making her smile.

"As I was saying," Helen went on pointedly, "I'm feeling a bit lost. I was always the lively one in my group of friends, the one that was spritely and bold, as you said, and it was thought that I lived an exciting life."

Jeremy watched in wonder as her throat worked on a swallow.

"I don't," she half-whispered. "I've never been as interesting as Margaret or as talented as Rosalind."

"For what it's worth," he replied, smiling kindly. "I think you are."

She didn't seem to hear him. "Margaret has lived everywhere. I've never even been to Brighton. Rosalind is dark, captivating, and musical. I can't carry a tune in a bucket, and my skills at the pianoforte haven't improved since I was twelve. All I am is rich."

"Oh, now that's a shame," Jeremy retorted.

She glared darkly, clearly ready to kick him again. "Stop that! I'd much rather be poor and pretty than rich and plain."

Plain? Jeremy scoffed once. "You are not plain, and you know it."

Helen rolled her eyes and folded her arms. "Rich and boring, then."

He smiled knowingly. "Not boring."

Her mouth screwed up in irritation, and she exhaled sharply. "Fine! Then rich and unhappy!"

Jeremy smiled at her, nodding his head. "Now, I think, we are getting somewhere."

The attempt at humor fell flat, but Helen smiled sadly. "I'm not anything like my friends, Jeremy, and because of that, I won't have anything that they have. Lovely, passionate, breathtaking marriages to their absolutely perfect counterparts, living happily forever no matter what else comes…" She shook her head slowly. "I wasn't supposed to be left behind."

"Who says you're left behind?" he murmured, moving closer to her. "Who told you that you wouldn't have what they do?"

Her eyes welled up with tears, and the sight arrested him. "It's obvious, isn't it?" she whispered.

Jeremy reached out and took one of her hands, tucked tightly against her, and smoothed his thumbs over the back of it. "Not at all obvious, or I wouldn't ask it. Helen…"

She looked up and met his eyes. "What?"

He felt his mouth curve up into a crooked smile. "There is no reason in the world why you can't have what your friends have. Why you can't have more, even. You speak as though the three of you ought to be perfectly identical in every way, your lives perfectly laid out in synchrony."

Helen sniffed weakly and made a soft sound of protestation.

He pressed her hand gently. "Helen… You're not like your friends, but why should that leave you behind?" He gave her a thorough look, smiling further. "I'm rather of the opinion that you are forging your own path, charging on ahead."

"It all sounds very brave when you say it like that," she replied, sounding stronger already.

"Isn't it brave?" he asked. "What you're doing?"

She shook her head at once. "Not in the least. Pathetic, weak, simple, lonely…"

"Well, it's always lonely at the top."

She stopped, giving him another look.

Jeremy chuckled and smoothed his thumbs over her hand again. "Stop comparing yourself with anybody else, Helen, love. You're not like any other person in this world, let alone any woman, or any of your friends. But I'll be damned if that means there is anything at all lacking in a single part of you."

He drew the hand he held to his lips, pressing a gentle kiss to her gloveless hand.

He caught her faint gasp of breath, and knew he'd gone too far, either in word, or in his attentions.

But he'd also be damned if he cared.

He laid her hand in her lap and slid back over to the far side of his seat, clearing his throat. "Quick, think of something else for us to talk about before I become yet another character to confuse you with."

Helen said nothing at all, and he glanced over at her as furtively as he could.

She stared at him with confusion, eyes wide and luminous, her full lips parted slightly.

He could have kissed her senseless and received a similar expression.

And suddenly, the idea had too much merit for his taste.

He shifted his attention out the window again. "It looks like rain. Fancy that, in England."

Helen coughed weakly. "What... what is your middle name, Jeremy?"

Jeremy grunted and felt himself smile, much to his relief. "Tiberius, unfortunately. Mother hoped it would make me the grand sort."

"Or at the very least scholarly..."

He glared at her in mock-consternation. "I'd like to kick you for implying I'm not."

Helen cocked her head at him. "So, do it."

Jeremy scowled. "I can't kick you first. It's unseemly."

Helen's lips quirked, and she seemed to laugh to herself.

Then he felt a kick against his shin, far less sharply than any before.

"There," she giggled, grinning broadly. "Have at."

And at that moment, Jeremy Pratt fell in love.

He stared at her as the sensation settled on him, and then retaliated the kick, much to the delight of his companion.

Chapter Seven

He loved her?

That was the worst sort of thing that could have happened to him during this whole affair. What a thing for an operative to have to admit, falling in love with the person he was tasked with protecting, minding, and escorting.

Lord above, Gent would have his neck...

If not several other parts of him.

Jeremy swallowed harshly, his hands gripping the reins he held more tightly. He'd jumped at the chance to venture outside when it was time to change the horses, eagerly inquiring if he could drive once more. Larkin had been only too pleased to have a rest, and Jeremy had been fully ready to move on when Helen had, yet again, heaved herself up into the seat beside him.

God was working a very twisted sense of torment on him, as though Jeremy had done the Almighty some dreadful wrong.

He couldn't immediately think of anything that ought to have earned him this, but he was no saint. The temptations warring within him now that Helen was sitting beside him were certainly evidence of that.

He exhaled slowly, trying to rein himself in as he could rein in the horses.

It would be fine. He'd only had a shock, a jolt of keen affection that had turned him slightly sentimental, perhaps maudlin, and he'd twisted that into thinking it was love. At that weak moment, he'd thought that the only way to describe it. But surely it wasn't.

It couldn't be.

Love was supposed to make one pine and moan, and ought to feel like bloody agony. He'd seen it in both Gent and Rogue when they'd been tossed about, and even Cap had shown signs of it, though he'd been a right coward running away from his wife in fear. They'd all suffered a great deal being in love.

Jeremy didn't feel as though he were suffering. He felt rather gleeful and euphoric, when he wasn't panicking.

Panicking wasn't pleasant, but it was to be expected under the circumstances.

He couldn't be in love.

So, the panic was uncalled for.

"I thought you said it was going to rain," Helen said in a teasing tone that sent sharp tingles into his toes.

Well, that was painful, so it could be love, he supposed.

Yet he smiled, just as he had done when she teased him before.

This was all very confusing.

"I said it *looked* like rain, Helen," he retorted sharply, noting how fine it was to say her name.

Had it been so pleasant before?

"Oh yes," Helen drawled with dramatics, "a fine clarification, that."

He turned his head to glare at her a little. "It changes the nature of your complaint entirely. I do not claim to know the weather, but I do know that when clouds look like this, it rains. Does it always do so? Of course not. But occasionally, it does."

"Ah," Helen mused softly. "So, there is one thing you cannot do?"

Jeremy chuckled and shook his head. "Cheeky. There are several things I cannot do."

Making sense of his own mind and heart was one of them.

Understanding the woman that he may or may not love was another.

Helen hummed, and he felt the vibration of it through his entire left side. "Well, we'd best not get into that. No sense in you castigating yourself just to prove a point."

"Thank you, that's very gracious," he muttered.

She laughed again, and he heard a symphony of sound in it.

He was going mad. Stark, raving mad.

He'd write a resignation letter the moment they reached the inn tonight.

If they reached the inn tonight.

"Tell me about John," Helen said suddenly, sighing as she leaned back slightly in her seat.

If she'd said she wanted a bedtime story, she couldn't have surprised him more.

He cleared his throat and adjusted his hold on the horses. "Why the hell do you want to know anything about John?"

Her soft giggle irritated him for the first time ever. "Well, you refuse to tell me anything about yourself, so I might as well ask questions about the Pratt brother with fewer secrets."

Jeremy barked a hard laugh. "Fewer secrets? My dear Helen, John has more secrets than the Knights Templar, the book of Isaiah, and Parliament all rolled into one. And he wouldn't do for you at all, anyway."

"Oh, for heaven's sake, Jeremy," Helen scoffed, "I've no desire to pursue your brother simply because I can't get a straight answer out of you. I know my preferred Pratt, and it's the one I actually know. I'm only being conversational."

He stiffened and kept his gaze fixed straight ahead, the grooves in the road creating invisible lines in his eyes as well. The trees they passed moved at the exact pace of his heart.

One... Two... Three... Four...

Exhale....

Lord, Jeremy...

Her voice in his head shook him as much as her words had, as though Helen were suddenly everywhere and everything.

Perhaps this was the madness of love after all.

But on the off chance it needed more room to grow...

"Your preferred Pratt, eh?" he repeated, letting himself smile as wryly as he ever had. "How many Pratts have you analyzed to find one so preferential?"

Helen sighed very dramatically, even for her. "So many. So very many. I'm quite exhausted by Pratts." She paused, then made an amused sound. "Well, perhaps not entirely."

Jeremy glanced at her out of the corner of his eye. "No?"

She looked over at him, and her full lips pulled back into a devious smile he instantly adored. "No. Not yet, at any rate."

"Yet?" he protested, even as his heart thudded against his ribs. "What do you mean, yet?"

Helen shrugged a shoulder. "Well, one never knows. I may tire of that one. If he remains mysterious, the attempts at improving the acquaintance might prove rather tiresome."

Now it was Jeremy who rolled his eyes and huffed a little, growling under his breath. "If you'd ask me questions, I might answer them satisfactorily."

"Who said I was talking about you?" she shot back. "I might be in love with your cousin Lester."

"I doubt that," he informed her at once. "Lester's got horrid teeth and a hump."

Helen kicked him as best as she could from beside him, and he, of course, reciprocated in kind.

Then, they both burst out laughing.

"Lord, Jeremy," she giggled breathlessly, far outstripping the version he'd heard in his head. "Tell me you don't truly have a cousin named Lester."

"I don't," he assured her. "At least not that I'm aware of. There was that rather bizarre uncle we lost track of, so I just might."

Helen shook her head and put a hand to her cheek. "Let us hope that, if he exists, he is hump-free and in possession of decent teeth."

"Indeed. I'd hate to be related to a degenerate cripple of that sort."

"Ugh, Jeremy…" she groaned. "What if he was a good-hearted man with the best soul?"

He made a face of consideration. "Then I'd procure him a lovely tower to live in so I could visit when I felt like being ashamed of myself and more fortunate for my circumstances."

"Jeremy!"

"What?" he asked with a laugh as he turned to her. "I'm no saint, I already told you, and you wanted honesty and answers."

Helen covered her face, laughing helplessly. "Lord…"

Jeremy chuckled, flicking the reins absently. "Yes, I'm afraid I tend to send people to prayers with some regularity. Always have done. Even those without religious tendencies."

She spread her fingers and gave him a derisive look through them. "I don't doubt that for a minute."

"Still think I'm the preferred Pratt?" he asked as he leaned towards her, quirking his brows with an unmistakable suggestion.

Helen's hands dropped, and she gave him a very frank look. Her eyes were so vibrant when she looked at him that way. They changed nearly to the color of the sky on a clear spring day; just as stirring, mesmerizing, and perfectly arresting.

"Yes," Helen said firmly, her eyes trained on his. "Yes, Jeremy, I do."

He grinned, breathless again, and wondered what pains of love anybody ever talked about.

Being in love was a rather pleasant sensation, in his estimation. And he greatly looked forward to feeling more of it.

Well, *that* was surely well done.

Admitting to Jeremy that he was the preferred Pratt, which was a ridiculous statement in and of itself, as she clearly only knew the one, but to actually admit that she preferred him…

Shameful behavior, that's what it was, and her mother would have been ashamed of her.

Proud, certainly, but definitely ashamed as well.

And yet, Helen Dalton did not feel the least bit ashamed, as her admittance had led to the most fun and flirtatious conversation they had perhaps ever had, including anything in London.

It amused her that she could catch little glimpses of the deeper aspects to Jeremy in their bantering, even if the topics were unimportant. It didn't matter to her, so long as she could continue to spend time with him, converse with him, see him as he was.

She believed him when he'd said that this was the true version of himself, and she was thrilled by the opportunity to know him as best as she could.

He was full of surprises.

Jeremy was a very intense man, which ought to have been clear from the days in London and in Society, but with all of the finery, it had been missed. Stripped of all of that, it was as clear as the road before them.

She loved that intensity.

He found humor in nearly everything, which was rather contagious, and spoke of the sort of outlook that would be rather encouraging for a person. Not that it was all good humor, for truly, some of the things were quite dreadful or downright shocking.

Which, of course, only made it more amusing.

He could say a great many things with his eyes, and she loved attempting to decipher what he was saying to her. She hadn't figured it out yet, but she did know he was saying a great many things.

She craved the day that she could see it all.

Lord, but being with Jeremy was a lark. Full of surprises, full of laughter, full of teasing, full of wonder and delight... It was so very full, and she wasn't sure she could bear it.

Lying in bed at the inn, she laughed at herself.

Of *course* she could bear it.

She was loving every minute of it and wondered if she might convince Mr. Larkin to take a more roundabout way to Leighton so the trip might take a bit longer.

Jeremy had driven them all the way to the inn, though he'd made them stop a full quarter mile away so that Helen could get back into the coach like the proper lady she was purported to be, and when they arrived, she called him Mr. Perry just to spite him.

That had given his eyes a look she was fully familiar with.

Delighted amusement, and bemused irritation.

He could hardly give her a proper retort when he was posing as her hired man, and he knew it.

Once within the inn, it was all very much the same as it had been the night before. Dinner in the taproom by the fire with laughter, though not as much as before, as this inn was more populated, but it was enjoyable and fun, and even Millie had smiled at one of Jeremy's quips. The memory of Jeremy's own smile at the sight would warm Helen's heart, toes, and knees until the end of time.

But then, just as before, he'd escorted her up the stairs, bowed at the door, and disappeared.

Again, Helen watched him disappear, taking an inordinate amount of pleasure in doing so, as he really was spectacularly built.

And he moved so very well…

Her cheeks flushed even now, though it had been at least one hour, if not two, since she'd watched him so shamelessly. And he'd certainly not seen her do anything of the kind, so really, there was not much to be ashamed of.

After all, she'd been watching him with as much intensity in London when he'd been so finely dressed and captivating, and she'd never been embarrassed about it before.

With as much intensity, perhaps, but without the same sort of emotions.

Without this excitement.

Without this… This…

Whatever this was.

Helen leaned her head further back against her pillow, laughing to herself. This was ridiculous. She couldn't sleep for thinking of Jeremy, and nothing had happened!

Nothing except finding that the man underneath all the pretenses was more exciting and captivating than the one she had been watching for almost a year.

And finding him far more to her liking.

And that he could rob her senses with a smile.

Or that the feeling of his foot across her shins would give her such warm and delirious sensations.

She obviously had no room to say so, but she wasn't sure that a kiss could do more for her than that.

She was willing to put that to the test, but it would take some convincing for Jeremy, she was sure. He wasn't even sharing details of his life with her; how could he possibly be prevailed upon to kiss her for her own insatiable curiosity?

Not that she didn't *want* to kiss him for the sake of kissing him. She did. Quite a lot.

But having no knowledge of the thing and no idea how to go about it, curiosity was the reigning motivation.

That seemed as good a place as any to start.

Tomorrow, she would see what she could do to bring that about. After the manner in which Jeremy had kissed her hand this morning, she rather thought she could find a way. After all, what man on earth would refuse a decently attractive woman's desire for a kiss if he had no objections to spending time with her unobserved?

Really, she was surprised it hadn't come about yet.

But then, Jeremy seemed to be a bewildering mix of a gentleman and a man who defied categorization.

There was no way to know where his opinions on any subject of propriety and morality were at any given time.

Helen groaned to herself and sat up, shaking her head. Thinking about and planning for kissing Jeremy was no way to try to sleep. She'd be up all night if she kept this up.

Flinging the cover off, she swung her legs over the edge of the bed, sliding her feet into slippers. She moved to the door and grabbed her wrap laying on the chair nearby, cinching it around her waist. It was best to ensure she would not shock any other patrons who might also struggle with finding sleep this evening, and there was no telling what a man with too much drink might take up with a vulnerable woman in a certain state of undress.

Jeremy would kill her if he knew what she was going to do.

She bit her lip on a nervous giggle and shook her head as she reached for the handle, turning it as quietly as she could. Though she could hear Millie snoring in the connecting dressing room, she had no desire to wake her with the sounds of her departure.

The door opened without a squeak, and Helen grinned at that.

But the grin faded as she took stock of her threshold.

There was a sleeping man just outside her door.

And not just any man.

Jeremy.

She gave him a thorough look up and down, making a note of distinctly feminine appreciation at his form, but forcing that aside for the moment.

What in the world was he doing there? He was sharing a room with Larkin. She had heard them specifically ask for two rooms when they had arrived. Yet here he was outside of her door, apparently settled in for the night.

It was too much, having just been dwelling on him and to now have him here, quite literally laid out before her.

"Lord, Jeremy," she said in as low a voice as she could while still being audible.

His eyes opened at once, and she wondered if he had truly been asleep at all there. "Helen."

She tilted her head at him. "What are you doing?"

"Trying to sleep."

Helen sighed, rolling her eyes. "Jeremy, get up. What are you doing on the floor? And why right before my door? I could have trampled you or kicked you on my way out."

He exhaled roughly and got to his feet, his hair delightfully disheveled. "I'd have just kicked you back and rolled over."

She grinned at the scene he painted in her mind and looked up at him curiously. "Jeremy," she said again, "what are you doing?"

He was suddenly sheepish and rubbed at the back of his hair in an oddly adorable fashion. "I just needed to make sure you were safe. When I wasn't with you."

Helen stared at him for a long moment. "So, you're sleeping outside of my door?"

He shrugged once, averting his eyes.

"Did you sleep there last night, too?" she asked, her voice dipping lower.

He nodded, keeping his gaze anywhere but on her.

"Jeremy…"

Slowly, his eyes rose to meet hers, and the intensity in them caught Helen in the middle of her chest.

Before she knew what she was doing, she moved two steps forward and took Jeremy's face in her hands, going up on tiptoe, and arching up to press her lips to his. He stiffened slightly, then slid one hand into her loose and unbound hair, the other reaching around her waist and pulling her close.

Helen's inexperience meant nothing anymore as Jeremy took complete control of the kiss, parting her lips easily with his own and showing her the way, gently and thoroughly dismantling any and all defenses she had ever thought herself to have. His lips teased her, far more effectively than his words ever had, and the insistent caresses sent a faint but stirring humming throughout her entire body. She clung to him, unable to sustain her own weight on her suddenly unsteady legs, her breath coming in faint gasps and sighs.

It was an eternity that their lips melded and fused, danced and grazed, and yet when Jeremy eased himself away with a low moan, Helen felt as though they had barely begun. They stood there for a wild moment, lips a faint breath from each other, panting unsteadily.

Jeremy smiled and laughed, the deep rumbling sound echoing through Helen down to her toes. "Now, what do you need, Miss Dalton?"

Helen released a gasping giggle and moved one of her hands to cover his in her hair. "Nothing. Nothing at all."

He leaned back and stooped to meet her eyes evenly, still grinning almost smugly. "You sure?"

She nodded, her lashes fluttering as his fingers stroked against her scalp. She smiled dreamily at him. "I can't even remember why I was going anywhere."

Jeremy chuckled, let his lips fall against hers once more, then stepped away, exhaling as he did so. "Then goodnight, Helen."

"Goodnight, Jeremy," she whispered, unable to stop smiling. She tucked her hair behind her ear, suddenly terribly shy, and turned for the door, shutting it in the most awkward way possible.

Then, as she leaned against the door, her heart finally decided it existed, pattered wildly, and seemed to ricochet off of every single one of her ribs.

Lord above, kissing was so much better than shin kicking. It wasn't even worthy of a comparison.

And Jeremy had... Jeremy was...

Helen bit her lip on the faintest squeal, and sank to the floor, drawing her knees to her chest, grinning like an absolute idiot. She covered her mouth as helpless giggles threatened to escape, and her shoulders shuddered with the delight of them.

A soft sound below her caught her attention and she looked down.

The tips of a few fingers had slid under the door, resting against the floor and seeming to hold a very faint tremor in them.

Helen stared at them, still grinning, only now her eyes began to prickle with tender tears. She sniffed them back, then sighed as she laid her fingers atop his, gasping quietly when they curled against hers.

An accompanying almost gasp echoed from the other side of the door.

She stared at their nearly-joined fingers for a number of heartbeats, then sighed again and leaned her head back against the door. "Lord, Jeremy," she breathed, her lips pulling back into the same dreamy smile they'd worn in the aftermath of his kiss.

His fingers brushed against hers once more in response.

Chapter Eight

$\mathcal{S}$ omehow, Helen managed to sleep, though her dreams had been a muddled delirium of colors, excitement, and soaring emotions that had only left her more exhilarated when she woke up.

Jeremy had been the key figure in those dreams, though the details were lost on her moments after waking.

Still, the anticipation of seeing him again was unbearable, and Helen had giggled and squealed the entire time Millie had assisted her as she dressed and prepared for breakfast. Millie had asked no questions, but her bemused smile told Helen that not many questions needed to be asked.

From Helen's perspective, there were many questions that needed to be asked, and many answers that she wanted to hear. But she would settle for the breathless anticipation she felt as she descended to the somehow empty taproom. Jeremy would be around somewhere, and she would know fairly quickly how to behave with him after such a night. His reaction to her would be key, and never had she been keener for observation.

And to be observed.

Again, she had chosen a less than ideal travelling gown, but there was nothing to be done about that. She knew full well how she looked in blue, and this particular powder blue highlighted her eyes in a rather fetching way.

Jeremy would appreciate that.

If he noticed.

Helen moved into the taproom, looking around curiously, and then she saw Jeremy striding in from the front, his attention elsewhere. Then, he looked over at her and stuttered a step before turning in her direction, his eyes fixed on hers, his mouth slowly curving.

She couldn't move as he approached, her pulse racing, her breath hitching, her cheeks flushing… She was a cacophony of sensation and emotion, hardly resembling herself at all. The thought occurred to her to say something, anything, but her lips hesitated to do anything at all.

Jeremy had no hesitation. He came directly to Helen, his chest heaving on an exhale, and reached for one of her hands, kissing the back of it very softly.

She barely had time to catch her breath before that hand was lifted to the back of his neck and he leaned down to capture her lips in a teasing, insistent kiss. Helen sighed into him, pressing him closer, catching his laughter in the kiss she was now actively, and eagerly, engaged in.

He pulled away, brushing his nose against hers. "Good morning," he murmured.

"I should say so," Helen breathed, grinning at him. "What was that for?"

Jeremy gave her a crooked smirk, his eyes dancing. "I wasn't sure if I dreamt it or not. I had to be sure."

She laughed and arched up to kiss him quickly. "Not a dream."

He leaned back and raised a brow. "You sure about that? This all feels rather dream-like."

Helen felt her cheeks heat again, and she averted her eyes. She was no shy and retreating miss, but something about him and his romantic words turned her inside out and upside down. Now she blushed frequently.

Jeremy laughed at her discomfiture and laced his fingers with hers, leading her over to a table where a fair breakfast spread lay.

He sat with her while she ate, keeping up a steady stream of conversation without any help from her, and making her smile so much her cheeks ached.

The day was young, and the road before them would be long, but Helen didn't care. She'd rather it was longer still, that her brother lived in Northumberland or some such, just to give her more time to feel this exhilaration and excitement, this giddy sense of wonder with this man who seemed incapable of releasing her hand today.

Never had she been so delighted to eat with only one hand.

Or do anything with one hand, for that matter.

Which was well, as hours later she was sitting in a carriage with Jeremy beside her, her hand still as nestled in his as it had been at breakfast. And all morning. And at luncheon.

And in the time that had passed since then.

They'd kept it as hidden from Millie as possible, which was far easier now that she was soundly asleep on her side of the carriage.

"She's not much of a chaperone for you, is she?" Jeremy mused as the pair of them stared at the slightly snoring Millie.

Helen nudged him hard. "Millie is lovely."

"I know that," he protested, "and I never said otherwise. All I meant was that she lacks a certain awareness that all chaperones ought to possess."

"Millie wasn't supposed to *be* a chaperone for me," Helen explained with all the patience in the world. "She is a companion, and a lady's maid, if none can be had. I'm really quite fond of her."

Jeremy groaned a little. "All very well, but in this instance, she would be better served being awake to ensure nothing untoward happened to you."

Helen glanced at Jeremy with a quirked brow. "Do you anticipate anything untoward occurring at this moment, Jeremy? Have I need of a chaperone?"

His mischievous grin was swift and endearing. "One never knows, which is why chaperones exist, I'd wager."

"Undoubtedly," Helen retorted wryly. "It would not surprise me if you were well-versed in all things chaperone."

Jeremy snorted softly. "Of course I am. I was a right scamp in my youth, and nothing irked me more than being supervised. It made no difference if it were supposed to induce me to behave or to keep a young lady from misbehaving, I chafed at them all. Not that I ever misbehaved with a young lady, as I never had any time to consider them properly. Too busy creating my own troubles. Poor John was always much better behaved, but he was so devoted to keeping me out of mischief that more often than not both of us were punished because his intervention appeared to be part of the trouble. Never mind that it always made things better than they could have been."

"It's a wonder he doesn't resent you." Helen laughed and tilted her head back to look up at him. "I would be furious with you for years if it had been me."

"Well, we almost never spoke at university," Jeremy informed her, his tone sardonic. "It took him a good three years to acknowledge me publicly, and even then, it was not fondly."

Helen shook her head against him. "Poor, friendless you."

Jeremy leaned away, looking at her incredulously. "I beg your pardon, whoever said I was friendless?"

She laughed and sat up. "Were you not?"

"Never!" he insisted firmly. "I have always been very popular, and very well thought of."

"Of course, do forgive me," she replied in a flat tone.

"No, I don't think I will."

Helen whacked his shin with her foot, and he responded the same.

"Shh!" he scolded, though their kicks hadn't made much noise. "Do you want to wake your trusted servant? She would be highly disapproving of our closeness, and of our gloveless hands touching, let alone doing so in such a forward way." He looked down pointedly at their hands, resting in Helen's lap.

"And then we would be chaperoned," Helen moaned dramatically. "More's the pity for our scandalous inclinations."

Jeremy sniffed dismissively. "Speak for yourself, Miss Dalton. I've never had anything of the sort. A true gentleman through and through."

She giggled and leaned against him, toying with their still-laced fingers. "Why didn't you say anything?" she murmured, though there was no danger of being overheard. "About this? Why did you never give me encouragement? You had to know I felt it."

Jeremy's lips pressed against her hair and his fingers brushed hers gently. "How could I? I was supposed to be a ridiculous fop, never serious about anything, and yet there you were… You, who could see past the charade and into my soul… It was the most disconcerting, terrifying sensation I've ever known. I had to be purely flirtatious with you because I was afraid of doing more. I couldn't ignore you, couldn't pretend I didn't notice you, didn't feel drawn to you, and I couldn't go without saying something. So, I flirted, sometimes shamelessly."

Helen covered their joined hands with her free one and rubbed his hand gently. "Oh, Jeremy…"

"I felt this the entire time, Helen," he told her, his voice rough and rumbling through her. "In every flirtatious, teasing moment, I felt whatever this is. It may have been flattering and ridiculous and the actions of a rogue or a rake, but everything I ever said to you or about you… was probably the sincerest I've ever been publicly in my life."

Tears prickled at the corner of Helen's eyes, and she lifted her head, her free hand moving to Jeremy's jaw, turning his face to hers.

"That is exactly what I hoped you'd say," she whispered, her voice catching at the end.

Jeremy's eyes darkened as they fixed on hers, and he leaned forward, pressing his lips to hers with surprising tenderness. He layered slow, lingering kisses upon her, everything unhurried and exquisite, and filled with some unspoken depth that made Helen shiver against him.

"Lord, Jeremy," she sighed, her lips catching on his.

He chuckled and cupped her cheek gently. "Do you even know what your voice does to me when it sounds like that?"

She grinned at him. "I'm inclined to investigate the claim."

"If we were not in a moving carriage rambling its way to York with a dozing servant nearby," he said as his lips moved across her cheek to her ear, "I'd fully encourage such an investigation."

Another shiver raced down her spine, and again her cheeks flushed. "Cursed circumstances that prevent such things…" she whispered.

"My sentiments exactly." His lips moved again, smiling as they pressed against hers.

Whatever might have followed was interrupted by a sudden shot ringing through the air, cracking loudly and the carriage jerking in response.

"What was that?" Helen gasped, clenching her hold on Jeremy.

But Jeremy wrenched away quickly, moving to the window, and

cursing harshly under his breath. "Hell's bells," he added to his already colorful statement.

"What is it?" Helen asked again, gripping her hands together anxiously.

Millie bolted awake and looked around absently. "What happened? What's going on?"

Another shot rang out, and Jeremy reached for the ceiling, yanking hard on the fabric, which tore away too easily and revealed a rifle stored above.

"Why is there a rifle in this coach?" she shrieked, bunching up in the corner.

Jeremy turned to face her, his expression taut and cold. "Stay in here. Get down, and don't scream." He looked at Millie hard. "Keep her here by any means necessary and stay down yourself."

"Aye, sir," Millie replied brusquely, nodding and moving over to Helen.

"Jeremy…" Helen whimpered, reaching for him.

He looked at her again. "Helen, stay here, and don't watch." Then he opened the door, rifle in hand, and climbed out of the rapidly moving coach.

"Jeremy!" Helen screeched as she heard another shot. "Come back!"

Millie wrapped her arms tightly around her, though Helen struggled. "Hush, my girl. Hush now."

Helen covered her ears and her face, her heart skittering at an impossible pace as the carriage moved faster, vainly trying to avoid imagining the danger the man she loved was putting himself in at this moment, or what could happen to him.

Or any of them.

He should have known this would happen. He'd been fully prepared for it two days ago. He'd been on alert, filled with anticipation, and all instincts finely tuned.

Then he'd been lulled into a state of delirium unlike anything he had ever felt, and he'd lost all sense of his purpose.

Now he was paying for it.

Jeremy gritted his teeth together as he climbed to the top of the carriage, which was no simple feat at the speed they were still moving. Larkin was an impossibly skilled hand at the reins, and the men riding up to the coach across the terrain would have to work hard to accomplish anything at all.

No one was taking this carriage hostage, and nothing and no one was going to be taken.

Jeremy hauled himself atop the coach, knocking aside the luggage in his way. Two trunks would provide adequate coverage for him, but the rest were simply obstacles, and he shoved them off of the coach completely.

"Steady, Larkin," Jeremy called as another shot echoed over their heads.

"Aye, Rook," came the brisk reply. "Steady as she goes."

Jeremy laid low, surveying the approaching riders, all masked. "I count four from the left."

"Aye, sir, an' two comin' up the right," Larkin reported.

That craned Jeremy's neck to the right of the carriage, and he swore under his breath again. "How did we miss them?"

Larkin shook his head once. "Didn't take the main roads, sir. Crossed terrain like they knew we had front and rear riders."

It was a chilling thought to consider that their entire trip had been compromised somehow, though what they thought Helen could give them was a mystery. She knew nothing of the League, and certainly had little enough in the way of possessions of value.

Which left Rook.

He ground his teeth together and reached for the pistol in his pocket. "Can you shoot and drive, Larkin?"

"Aye, sir, both blindfolded an' while whistling 'God Save the King'."

Jeremy smiled slightly. "Skips taught you well. I'll settle for the skills alone and leave the rest for a less demanding time. Take the right side."

"Aye, Rook!"

Grateful his guns were already loaded, Jeremy took up aim and fired the rifle in the direction of the riders, hitting one in the shoulder and scattering the rest.

With no one to reload for him, the rifle was now only good for its bayonet and butt as a weapon, so he laid it aside and fired his pistol at the nearest rider.

Larkin fired his, but Jeremy couldn't see how his aim had been. He aimed at the rider making for the back of the coach, and hit him squarely in the side, grunting in satisfaction as he heard the pained cry.

"Larkin!" he called. "Did you stash more firearms? We need about four more men and a dozen guns."

"Aye, sir, under the hat boxes you'll find another two, but that's it," Larkin bellowed back as he released another shot. "Not Gent's horses, ye bleeding frog lover!"

Jeremy heard the crash of horse and rider and felt the thrill that called him back to his army days. "Good one, Larkin!" he praised as he fired off the second shot from his pistol, forcing a rider to duck.

Larkin whooped and flicked the reins. "Running out of options, Rook. Bit more action on the way!"

Jeremy laid himself flat as another shot came near, and he cursed. One rider down, two injured, but possibly still viable. Only four more shots, if that, from the remaining guns. Their reinforcements wouldn't arrive in time to be of much use, though they would have heard the shots and been hastening towards them.

But until then…

Jeremy lay on the roof, ignoring the sound of the snapping reins, of the terrified whimpers he could hear within, of everything but the horse hooves coming from the side and behind them.

Wait… wait… wait…

He surged up and thumped the nearest rider across the head with the butt of the rifle as he rode up, sending him sprawling into the grass.

"*J'ai vécu!*" the one to Jeremy's left bellowed, sending a ripple of fury and disgust down his spine. He shoved aside the hat boxes and found one of the remaining pistols, then rolled to his side and met the man's furious eyes.

Without hesitation, Jeremy fired both shots into the man's chest, turning away before he could see the body fall. He threw the now-empty pistol at the head of another rider, who dodged it easily, though he winced as the blood continued to seep from his earlier shoulder wound. The one he'd hit before still lay in the grass, the one he'd stabbed was close to falling off his horse from the loss of blood, and the other was fast approaching the back of the coach, his eyes fixed on it.

Just then, another shot rang out, this one hitting the back of the coach, sending the women inside screaming.

"The hell you just did!" Jeremy barked, raising his head a little. He reached for the last pistol, pulled the empty rifle's strap over his shoulder, and shoved himself off of the coach. He landed directly onto the horse beside him, behind the rider, who reached back with a knife and sliced Jeremy's arm easily.

Jeremy winced and jammed his pistol into the shoulder wound of the man before him, far worse in the back than in front, and the rider screamed, his mask not doing anything to muffle the sound. Jeremy shoved him off and watched as he rolled to the ground, barely missing the wheels of the coach.

Jeremy urged the horse further, looking up at Larkin. "Diversionary tactics, Larkin! I've got this!"

"Aye, Rook!" he replied, immediately changing his hold on the reins and sliding the horses in Jeremy's direction.

Jeremy reined his horse in sharply, letting the coach move on the road. He dropped back behind the coach and found the way empty. He frowned at that, his eyes scanning the surrounding area.

"Where are you?" he hissed, leaning down closer to his stolen horse. "Where...?"

A piercing scream came from the coach, and Jeremy jerked his horse to the right side of it, where the remaining rider had a pistol pointing into the carriage.

His vision suddenly held a distinctly red sheen, and he urged his horse faster, harder, gaining on them all.

If Larkin could veer the coach again...

As if an order had been given, the coach suddenly weaved to the right, forcing the rider to readjust, the gun not quite so steady.

"Come on, boy," Jeremy murmured to the horse. "Come on. Be

a hero."

The horse obeyed and raced even harder. Larkin's efforts forced the rider off the road entirely, and his horse struggled with the rougher terrain. The pistol no longer pointed at the coach, and the rider's frustration was evident in his frantic whipping of his horse.

Jeremy grinned and pulled closer and closer, coming between the rider and the coach with ease. If he wanted to intimidate the women again, he would have to do so through Jeremy.

And that wasn't happening.

He was drawing closer to the side of the man, who oddly did not turn to fire at him, which made Jeremy wonder if his gun had any shots left at all. He slung the rifle from his shoulder and hefted it up, then shoved it forward into the back of the rider, who arched up and reined in his horse just enough with his pain.

Jeremy lunged for him, wrenching him off his saddle and tumbling with him to the ground. They landed hard, but Jeremy was quick to pull out his pistol, beating the man across the face with it before pointing it directly at his heart.

The man stirred in agitation, spat blood, and jutted his chin out. "*J'ai…*" he began, but Jeremy grabbed the bayonet and pressed it into the man's thigh.

"Don't you dare," he hissed. "I am so bloody sick and tired of that stupid phrase, which you're probably too ignorant know the translation of, and it's grating on me."

His victim made an odd screeching noise as the bayonet pressed further into his leg but made no further attempt to speak.

"Wise notion." Jeremy whistled loudly, and the carriage pulled to a slow halt. "Larkin!" he called. "Come help me with this rodent. Bring something to bind him with."

Larkin jumped down from his perch and jogged over, his glower rather thunderous.

And no wonder, given they'd been attacked by Faction supporters and nearly lost their horses, of whom he'd become especially fond, not to mention the danger to the women, let alone Gent's coach.

There was a great deal to be angry about.

Jeremy held the gun steady on him while Larkin bound his hands and feet with rope, surprising Jeremy by also including a loop around the man's neck.

"Jus' in case he gets any ideas," Larkin informed Jeremy with a grunt.

There was no arguing with that.

"Jeremy?"

He turned at the weak call and saw Helen stepping out of the carriage, her hair completely disheveled, her cheeks tear stained, and her eyes round.

Groaning, he gave Larkin the pistol and strode over to her.

She shook from head to toe, but her arms reached out for him as he neared her, and he swept her up easily, clutching her to him.

"Oh, love, I'm sorry," he murmured, his words nearly lost in her hair. "I'm so sorry."

Sobs came tumbling from her lips as she clung to him, fisting his shirt in her hands. She rambled incoherently, burying her face into his shoulder and shuddering even in his hold.

"Helen, I'm so sorry." He shook his head against her, rubbing circles on her back.

"Stop apologizing and make the trembling stop," she ordered shakily.

He chuckled and pulled her in close. "You're safe now, love. I promise. I've got you."

Helen sighed against him, nuzzling as she did so. "That's my only comfort at this moment."

Jeremy smiled, pulling back to cup her face. "Are you all right? Physically?"

She nodded, her lashes fluttering as her hands moved to grip his wrist. "Physically, yes."

He nodded in return and kissed her hard, feeling the pains of the danger she'd been subjected to on his account, and what he knew must follow.

Helen broke off first, which seemed telling, but her eyes were keen as she looked at him. "Your arm is bleeding!" she screeched.

Oh, damn, he'd forgotten about that. He glanced at it and shrugged. "It's fine. Just a graze, it won't even scar." He stooped to meet her eyes better. "You're not going to faint at the sight of blood, are you?"

She sputtered in indignation. "I've never fainted in my life, Jeremy Pratt, and your little bleeding scratch is not about to break that record."

A show of life and spirit. Good. He needed to see her vibrant and alive, unperturbed by their escapade, by the danger, by fear…

He needed…

"What was that, Jeremy?" Helen asked him, now rather somber. "Why were they shooting at us?"

He shook his head and stepped away, smiling a little. "It's not your concern, I'll see to it. I'll sort it all out."

Her brow furrowed deeply. "But…"

"You'd best see to Millie now, love," he overrode, nodding towards the coach. "I doubt she's as brave as she appears." He didn't wait for her to do so, and turned away, walking back over to Larkin, who kept a steady watch on their prisoner.

Larkin looked at him, his expression set. "Not a bleeding word, Rook. I've asked very nicely."

Jeremy grunted once. "He'll talk. One way or another, we'll make him." He looked down the road, sighing shortly. "The riders will be upon us soon, and they can take up minding him until I can do a proper interrogation. Until they do, I'd best fetch what I can of Miss Dalton's belongings." He looked back at Larkin, resignation settling over him. "It's going to be a long night, Larkin, and we'll need to push the horses as far as we can and stop as little as possible."

"Aye, Rook. I take your meaning."

Jeremy nodded, struggling to swallow. "With any luck, we'll be in York tomorrow, and all this will be behind us."

He hoped his own words were true.

He needed it behind him.

He doubted it would be.

Chapter Nine

$\mathcal{T}$he solitude was both deafening and chilling. Hours of not conversing with Helen, not seeing her, not thinking of her…

Well, he could not completely escape that one.

Helen had been his entire focus and purpose for some time now, despite the other things that occasionally tried to replace her.

He'd loved her, for pity's sake.

Loved.

Had loved.

He couldn't think of it any other way. There was too much that had to come between them now, and giving her up was the only way to ensure her ultimate happiness. Such a short, blissful time together, and yet the end was upon them. From ecstasy to agony in less than a day, all for a bloody painful purpose.

Necessary, but painful.

Helen would never see it that way, but he could not bother with sparing her feelings now. Not with everything that had occurred, not with so much at stake. There was no time for explanation or gentleness, or anything remotely resembling the easy nature of their venture prior to this.

They needed to get to York, see to her safety, and investigate the newest cycle of events before any more time passed.

Jeremy sat beside Larkin on the driver's seat, not seeing anything around him, his mind whirling.

They'd changed horses twice now, and each time, the change had been swift and efficient. Nothing had been unpacked, no greetings had been made, and there had been no relieving or refreshment for any but the horses. They had made no attempt to continue travelling inconspicuously, given the attack, so the contacts and associates now fully escorted them rather than riding at a distance.

He didn't care what Helen thought of that, or what questions she had. Her safety was paramount, not her curiosity.

Explanation was impossible.

Those hadn't been just any highwaymen looking for a fortune, and he could not pretend otherwise.

J'ai vécu. Even now, the words chilled him. His fingers itched to throttle the one he'd managed to capture, demand to know what he knew, what any of them knew, and what the hell they were trying to find. How did they know about Hal? How had they known about him? How had they known exactly when to attack and where? And in what manner? They'd not used the main roads, so their riders ahead and behind had known nothing of them and had only heard the guns.

No one should have been able to execute an attack so perfectly.

It was astonishing that they hadn't been more successful. By all accounts, they should have been, which led Jeremy to believe that they were hired hands and not skilled operatives themselves.

One operative, an asset, and two cowering women should not be enough to put such a group off.

Granted, Jeremy was rather skilled in all things combat, and Larkin was a skilled shot, but even then, it shouldn't have played out the way it did.

And that made him more nervous.

Who was to say that another attack was not imminent? Even now, others could be lying in wait for them, and the outcome could be different.

The motivation was unclear, but there was no time for analysis when innocents were at risk. Once Helen and Millie were safely ensconced in York, they could look at the problem from all aspects and angles. Jeremy would interrogate their captive with all the intensity and thoroughness such tasks required, then he would pass him, and the information, off to the others, who would take him back to London for the League to deal with.

At which point, Jeremy would continue on to Cheshire, and all that needed to happen there.

There was no time for the romantic falderal he'd been enjoying of late, and he should have known that. He had been tasked with seeing Helen to York, and then continuing his investigation into Trace's work. Everything else had to be secondary for the good of the League, London, and England itself. There was far too much work and danger for him to forget all of that. His life was not his own, and nor was his attention.

It couldn't be.

It wasn't fair to Helen, given what he'd been doing, but he couldn't apologize for it. If she understood, she would see the wisdom in his actions. But she could not understand, and there was no time to explain it.

So out here he sat, rain pouring down on them, pretending he didn't ache everywhere.

The horses pummeled the road in their haste, barreling them all down the lane at the rate of a mail coach, and their accompanying riders kept easy strides. No one said a word.

There was no need to.

Jeremy winced as he recalled Helen's face at their first exchange after the attack. She'd looked concerned and bewildered, still so lovely even in her distress that his heart had lurched painfully within him. She'd opened her mouth to say something, and he'd turned away, forcing himself to ignore everything about her as they made quick work of changing horses. Orders had been barked to the others, and he didn't even care that they all called him Rook within her hearing.

She could think whatever she liked about him; it made no difference anymore.

There was no hiding her wounded expression at their second exchange. She hadn't tried to speak to him again, but her eyes had spoken volumes.

He'd worked even more brusquely then, needing to avoid her eyes and hurt more than ever before. Larkin had seen to securing food for the ladies, as it had been hours since anything had been had, but Jeremy hadn't dealt with anything in that regard. He'd been too busy conferring with their riders on the appropriate maneuvering for the darkness of the roads, anticipating more danger than they would probably have.

It was an adequate excuse and distraction.

And now they would exchange again.

He prayed she would be sleeping now. His fatigue was beginning to set in, and his worry and guilt over her could incline him in a direction he dared not proceed.

"Inn ahead, Rook," Larkin grunted.

Jeremy nodded, seeing the lights. "See to the horses. I'll fetch us warm drinks and a brick for the ladies. Then I'll drive, and you take a rest."

Larkin gave him a sidelong look. "You sure, Rook? You've not slept."

"No, nor will I," he replied firmly. "Not until this is done."

There was no response from the man beside him, and he was grateful Larkin was not more inquisitive.

It made him an ideal traveling companion.

Larkin called their arrival at the inn, and a few drowsy lads sprang forward. Jeremy whistled once, and the riders spread out a little, dismounting as they reached the inn. Drinks were brought to them, and they stretched their backs, checked their weapons, and assisted with the horse changing.

Jeremy strode into the inn and requested a hot brick from the innkeeper, who took one look at his set expression and dashed off.

That didn't happen often. Rogue was the one with a glower to make gargoyles weep, and Cap had the authoritative persona to make even the unruliest obey. Even Gent could look imposing if he were so inclined.

Jeremy had never been in possession of intimidating expressions, but every now and again, he managed well enough.

The brick, wrapped in linen, was brought in and handed to him. He took the edges of the fabric in hand, nodded at the innkeeper and tossed coins on the desk. Before he could think about it too much, he went back out into the rain, walked directly to the carriage, and opened the door.

Helen looked at him blearily, her hair almost completely down around her shoulders. He fixed his gaze to the floor of the coach before he would be tempted to open his mouth, and set the brick down, pushing it across the floor close to Helen and Millie's feet.

"Thank you," Helen murmured as she slid her feet from her unlaced boots and rested them upon the brick.

The weak tone of her voice caused a lump to rise in his throat, and he swallowed once.

Damn. He wasn't supposed to feel anything at all, and suddenly he wanted to leap into the coach and haul her into his arms. But he only nodded, closed the carriage door, and moved to climb back up to the seat where Larkin was already waiting.

"Sure you want to take the reins, Rook?" Larkin asked, looking unconvinced.

Jeremy held out a hand, sighing as the rain intensified and began to pour down the brim of his hat and down his back. "Yes. I need the distraction."

Larkin gave him the reins, nodding once. "Aye, Rook. If you insist."

"I do," he grunted in return as he set the horses in motion. "Get some rest if you can, Larkin. It's going to be a long night, and a long day tomorrow. And then the real work will begin."

Despite his words, Larkin gave no indication that he would do any such thing, and his eyes constantly scoured the dark and damp horizon.

York was still a way off, but pushing through the night would get them there soon enough.

That had to be his goal and his aim.

Helen would be safe, and he could move on.

He'd have made her miserable eventually as it was. He had no notion how to be a proper gentleman in truth, or how to trust anyone with the sort of vulnerability she would require. No polite or staid marriage would do for Helen Dalton, should she have ever wanted something so far-fetched with him as it was. She would want absolutely everything a man could give and would give just as much of herself in return.

Jeremy could never do that. He could not offer up the whole of himself without reservation, and that sort of holding back would wear on the relationship eventually. The strain between them would build and build until it ripped apart entirely, reducing everything they had been to shreds of memory and emotion. He could not bear to do that to her, or to himself. To endure such agony would destroy more than the ties that bound them.

Helen would have been unrecognizable after that, and he refused to subject her to it.

Jeremy flicked the reins harder, pushing the horses faster still.

York needed to come sooner rather than later. He needed physical distance from Helen if he had any chance of emotional distance.

Or any distance at all.

Whatever was between them, it needed to end, for the good of everyone.

Each change of teams at inns along the way forced another small crack into Helen's heart, and it was all she could do to keep her composure.

She was cold, she was wet, and she was exhausted. The rain had been incessant, and though she had not disembarked often throughout the night, she had done so enough to dampen nearly every inch of her, and the coach did nothing to dry her out. The further they went, the colder she became, and the more uncomfortable.

But nothing could be more uncomfortable than how she felt inside.

The Jeremy she had come to adore more completely than she had ever thought possible was gone, and in his place was yet another stranger. Not Mr. Pratt, not Jeremy, but a cold, firm man with no thought but the task before them. There were no smiles, no fond expressions, no glimmers of mischief or flirtation in his eyes. If she looked too closely, she was sure there wouldn't even be a distinguishable color to those eyes. He was all hard angles and stern looks, nothing to indicate warmth or regard in any respect.

Yet throughout the night and in the early morning, at every stop, he had seen that the warming brick had been exchanged for a fresh one, that food was at hand, and their welfare seen to. The food she had expected, the welfare a given, but that warming brick… Every single time he appeared to remove the brick only to appear with a blessedly fresh one, she found a small inkling of hope.

He never looked at her for long, and never said more than a few words, but she felt warmed by the brick as though he had taken her hand in his.

She tended to forget that in the course of the uncomfortable coach ride, but she was reminded with every brick exchange.

They had stopped every three hours or so, though she was convinced it had been four once or twice. The poor horses would be weary to the bone in their haste, not to mention the exhausted and soaked riders. Larkin and Jeremy alternated driving, and it seemed to her that the carriage and teams moved just a little faster with Jeremy at the reins.

Helen didn't understand why they had to be quite so pressed in their efforts. Clearly there was danger, but now they had accumulated seven or eight additional riders that surrounded them, though she had no idea where they had come from. No one would attack such a guarded coach, and they were a right spectacle for anyone to see.

It didn't make any difference, she supposed. It had been clear from the start that they would not stop until they reached Leighton, and so she had said nothing on the subject. Jeremy had said from the beginning that he needed to be sure she was safe, and he had been tasked with protecting her. Why shouldn't he wish that task to be completed with some expediency?

Could he blame himself for the attack on the coach? It was a ridiculous thought. He could not have known that highwaymen would attack them, nor could he have prevented it. And he had seen to their protection himself without needing much assistance.

Despite his telling her not to watch, she had done so every chance she could. He had been a magnificent sight, moving with certainty and authority, a creature of power and danger that stirred an excitement within her. Fear in abundance, naturally, but not necessarily at what she was seeing. Fear that she would lose him. That it would not be enough. That, for all his incredible skill, she would be parted from him in some way.

Questions had risen in her mind one after another until questions were all she could think, and yet she had no answers. Worse than that, she may have lost him after all.

She'd be well on her way to believing she had were it not for the exchange sometime in the early morning hours. Millie had been sound asleep, as she usually was in the coach, and Helen was not. The coach had rolled to a stop, and she'd heard the riders dismounting, the sounds of teams being changed, and she waited in anticipation for the door to open.

It had moments later, and Jeremy had reached for the brick, sliding it towards him without looking at her. Water ran down his hat in great sheets, and she could see clearly that he was soaked through. He had handed the brick off to one of the riders, who had taken it inside. Then Jeremy had pushed his hat back just a little and almost sagged against the coach. His eyes had shifted to Helen, and he seemed surprised that she was awake, let alone staring back at him.

This time, he hadn't looked away. He'd kept his gaze steady on her. "Are you all right?" he'd inquired, the words polite, the tone rough.

No, she'd nearly said, but she'd opted for a short nod.

"Do you need anything?" he'd pressed, something almost hungry in his eyes now.

You. Helen had swallowed once as a shiver raced across her skin. "N-no," she'd managed. "Thank you." Then, against her better judgment, she'd cocked her head and asked, "Do you?"

His lips had quirked slightly, and he'd shaken his head slowly. "No. Though I could do without the rain."

That had made Helen smile, which had made him stiffen, and then he'd turned away.

She'd almost wept at that, but he'd returned moments later with the fresh warming brick and an additional blanket, half climbing into the coach to set the brick beneath her feet and lay the blanket across her legs.

His fingers had brushed her leg and she'd felt the jolt of sensation race into her heart.

"Thank you, Jeremy," she'd whispered.

He'd paused, but his eyes had never lifted to hers again. A nod was the only answer she'd received, and then he'd left the coach, closed the door, and the carriage had rolled on as it had done before.

He hadn't said a word to her since.

Now, the sky was beginning to lighten, and a sinking feeling washed over Helen.

Somehow, she knew there would be no more changing horses, no more warming bricks, and no more chances to glimpse the man she had fallen in love with.

York would be here all too soon, and there would be nothing left of the whirlwind venture with him.

Millie snored against the wall opposite her, but Helen only dozed fitfully, as she had the rest of the night. The pounding of the horse hooves all about her made for an odd percussion amidst the sound of the pouring rain and the thunder, somehow both soothing and jarring at the same time.

Her emotions echoed the sensation. She had no desire to be at Leighton now, she acknowledged, as she stared out of the window at the gloomy countryside. She'd never wanted to be anywhere less than Leighton and York. Yet she was desperate to be free of this carriage, and away from Jeremy.

Jeremy as he was now, not the man she had known before.

The man she had kissed with such exuberance, who had left her breathless and giddy, would have changed everything. She would have gone anywhere for and with him, no matter the danger, length, or inconvenience. This man who barely spoke a word, who was distant and unfamiliar, held nothing for her but pain and anguish.

Yet he resembled her Jeremy often enough to make her ache.

To be away from the pain would be a blessed relief, but Helen suspected that, once away from him, the pain would only increase. To have known his affection and felt his tenderness and then have it ripped from her would be a torment she couldn't bear to endure.

But what choice did she have?

She whacked her head against the wall of the coach in frustration. Cursed girl, it was her own blasted fault for being desperate to be away from London for a time. None of this would have happened if she'd had an ounce of backbone and stayed with Rafe and Margaret. She would never have had to endure the journey to York with the man she'd been trying to escape. Then she would never have known just how much more there was to discover about him, and how much more to love.

Or that he had returned her feelings.

Or that he could make her dream unspeakable dreams.

Or that he would be even more perfect for her than she'd already believed.

Or…

Helen closed her eyes on a wash of tears. Lord, how she'd dreamed, even in this coach in her fitful dozing. Dreams of a life with Jeremy, of their wedding, of their children, of the mad, passionate flirtation they would engage in across London's ballrooms… All lay shattered now.

But it had not ended yet. There was nothing to say that once they arrived at Leighton, he would not be returned to her.

She could not manage the hope that such an event would occur.

The coach suddenly turned down another road, and Helen's eyes sprang open. The city of York was before them, and she recognized the impressive edifice of York Minster in the distance.

Five miles.

Five miles was all that stood between them and Leighton. And the end of anything and everything she had hoped for her and Jeremy.

This dream that had turned into a nightmare.

"Hush, Helen," she hissed to herself. "It's not so bad as all that. Don't be dramatic without purpose."

Millie suddenly stirred noisily. "What was that, miss?" she asked as she righted herself, her eyes puffy and unfocused. She wrapped her shawl more tightly around her and peered out of the window. "Oh! York! Well, that's a pleasant surprise. I cannot wait to be out of this ruddy coach. If you'll forgive the impertinence, miss."

Helen waved that off instantly. "Of course. This is not a usual trip, and we have endured a great deal."

Millie nodded almost frantically. "If it weren't for Mr. Pratt, I don't know what might have become of us."

Helen forced herself to smile and nod, then returned her attention to the window, pretending to watch the scenery.

It was true, no matter how she might have hurt by the fact now. Jeremy had saved them all, and quite spectacularly. If anyone else had been hired by Rafe to escort her, she was fairly certain a great many things would have been stolen, and someone amongst them would have been injured, if not killed.

Yet they were all well and whole, and not even a hair pin had been lost.

The man she had thought about nearly constantly for a year, and with more intensity over the last few days, had saved her life. Had saved all of them.

At this moment, she felt no thrill at the admission.

Only pain.

Millie said nothing else as they rambled on, keeping busy by setting herself to rights, rearranging her appearance and the like, and Helen was grateful for her distraction.

Leighton would be bustling with the children in their excitement, and Helen had absolutely no interest in taking part in that. She wanted peace and quiet, a place of refuge and reverie. A haven for her heart, and a balm for her soul. She doubted Charles, or his wife Fanny, would be able to provide her that, but at least they were not intrusive people.

Usually.

Where a handsome man of convenient availability was concerned, however, they might make an exception. Pity the distance between Helen and said available man was growing as vast as the miles they travelled.

Before she knew it, the gates of Leighton were before them, and the cold marble exterior of the house looked more haunting in the bleak expanse of clouds and rain than she'd ever dreamed possible. A few windows were lit, no doubt servants preparing for the day, but other than that, there was no sign of life.

All too apt for the current situation.

The coach pulled around the wide circle drive, and, to Helen's surprise, servants descended from the house quickly, followed by her brother and Fanny, both dressed, albeit not formally.

Both looked exceptionally relieved.

The door to the coach opened and Jeremy stood there, nearly as relieved as her brother seemed to be.

Helen gave him a questioning look. "I didn't think we were

expected so soon. Or so early."

Jeremy nodded once. "I sent one of the riders on ahead straightaway. They were alerted to the situation hours ago, and no doubt have been anxiously awaiting our arrival." He held out a hand to help her down, and she stared at it for a heartbeat or three.

He hadn't helped her down during any of the stops previously. She hadn't touched his hand in ages.

She'd forgotten what it felt like.

She swallowed hard and placed her hand in his, the other hand clenching at her wrap and coat. Jeremy's hand closed about hers, his fingers curving too familiarly against hers as he helped her down.

Helen's legs shook beneath her, and she gasped as they nearly gave way, her other hand flying to Jeremy's wrist instinctively. His other arm latched around her at once, bearing her up with ease.

"Steady," he murmured, the gentle tone somehow strengthening her legs and stilling her slight tremors. "I've got you. Don't faint."

"I don't faint," Helen reminded him in a would-be firm tone, glaring at him briefly.

His smile, though fleeting, soothed her heart, and she hesitantly kicked his shin.

His eyes remained on hers, his throat worked in a swallow, and then, very faintly, he tapped his foot against hers.

Helen's eyes filled with tears at once and a sob caught in her throat. "Jeremy..."

"Helen!"

Jeremy's hold on her suddenly vanished and Charles came to her, holding her tightly. Helen could barely feel him, and her eyes hunted for Jeremy again, though he was now helping Millie down.

Charles suddenly thumped Helen on the back and pulled away, looking her carefully over. "Dearest, are you well? You're not hurt, are you? Blimey, you look like you've been through hell."

"I have," she managed, her voice catching.

Charles rubbed her arms, smiling sadly. "We've been so worried. Fanny hardly slept for her anxiety. But you're here now, and I've had a bath ordered for you, as well as breakfast."

Helen nodded absently, watching Jeremy move to the back of the coach to help the others pull the luggage down.

Too many things. Why had she packed so many things? It was ridiculous how much she had thought necessary to bring, and now he was wasting time pulling it all off the coach. If she'd brought less, they might not have been such a tempting target for the highwaymen. Jeremy might have had an easier time as he'd been atop the coach protecting them. They might have…

"Oh, Helen!" Fanny gushed as she pulled Helen into a warm embrace. "Look at the state of you!" She shook her head, her loosely braided dark hair bouncing with the motion. "You'll likely catch cold, so I'll send for the doctor this afternoon once you've rested. Come."

Helen resisted being tugged away, straining for one more look from Jeremy, one more smile, one more… anything.

"Our gratitude, Mr. Perry, knows no bounds," Charles said as he moved to Jeremy, hand extended.

Jeremy straightened and took his hand, shaking firmly. "Unnecessary, Mr. Dalton. I'm only glad we were able to see your sister here safely after all she's been through. If you'll send word to Lord Marlowe of her safe return, I'd be most grateful."

"To be sure," Charles replied, nodding. "But will you not return directly?"

Jeremy shook his head, studiously avoiding Helen's gaze. "I've other assignments to see to before returning to London." He smiled a bit. "Hopefully involving less exertion than the one I've just completed."

Helen balked at the words. Assignment. Exertion. Completed.

None of those words were flattering, and none gave her comfort.

Charles shook his hand once more. "Thank you all the same, Perry. Truly."

Jeremy nodded, and let his hand drop. Then, and only then, did he look at Helen.

She stared at him, hoping, waiting…

He bowed perfectly, then straightened. "Miss Dalton."

She opened her mouth to reply, but no words were there.

Fanny encircled her shoulders with an arm, and turned her towards the house, and this time Helen let her.

But she glanced over her shoulder to see Jeremy watching her still, and then he moved to the free horse being held in place by one of the riders, mounted easily, and rode out of the gates of Leighton. Without looking back.

Chapter Ten

The innkeeper had given them an hour. Just one. Not because he disapproved, but because it was all the privacy he could ensure.

Jeremy didn't mind.

One hour was plenty for a man properly trained.

Yet he had sat here for a good twenty minutes, arms folded sitting in a chair, staring off at nothing.

He hadn't slept in almost three days, and he was beginning to feel the effects of it. His mind wasn't as sharp as it usually was in times like these, his body ached without exertion, and everything seemed to come a little slower than it ought to. But he was used to working under extreme circumstances, and this was extreme.

It occurred to him that he could have taken respite in York after leaving Leighton yesterday, but at the time, he could only think of getting away and getting on with things.

Now he was here, getting on with things, except...

Well, nothing was happening.

The contacts and assets all sat in the taproom, waiting for his orders and instructions, and they'd set the room up perfectly. They were undoubtedly ready to return to their lives and regular assignments, and he was ready to let them. He had plenty of other things to be seeing to, including some sort of rest and recovery. He could hardly proceed to Cheshire as sleep deprived and foggy as he currently was, given what his investigation must entail.

But he would freely admit to being a bit of a coward where sleep was concerned at present.

He feared what dreams would descend if he drifted off.

And yet, he craved them.

Dreams might hold memories of Helen, glimpses of her as she had been days ago before the attack, imagined scenes of the journey as it might have been, should the attack never have happened, or visions of the future. Or they could turn darker, nightmares of a more intense attack, a bloodier battle between them, and Helen being a victim strewn across the road while he was helpless to save her. Beyond any of that, they could be as desolate as his reality was, a sound and dreary shade of grey in absolutely everything, with Helen being weary and worn, near to tears but never crying, her pale eyes paler with disappointment and pain…

Jeremy had heard of the nature of opium, and how laudanum could give one dreamless sleep. Suddenly, it seemed a bliss beyond compare to experience such a thing.

He could drink himself into an oblivion, he supposed, but that had other ramifications that he didn't feel inclined to endure, especially given he needed to travel again shortly. And travel decently far.

But he'd never been given a deadline, so who would know if he'd decided to take a brief holiday to forget what he'd just left behind?

"Look, are you going to get on wi' it, or no?"

Jeremy lifted his gaze just enough to make eye contact with the bound man in the chair across from him.

He was a stocky fellow, with a thick Northern accent, which was almost amusing, considering he was purported to be a French sympathizer. He could even be a lowland Scot, perhaps, and the thought of the grizzled chap in a kilt was enough to almost dispel Jeremy's gloom.

Almost.

Jeremy reached into his boot and pulled out a switchblade, then bent over to pick up a large shard of wood from one of the logs near the fireplace. Slowly, deliberately, he began whittling the narrow end into a point, looking up at his captive every now and then.

The man watched Jeremy's knife as it easily and neatly pared the wood.

"*Pouvons-nous commencer?*" Jeremy asked him, keeping his tone mild and friendly.

His prisoner's eyes widened, and his throat worked on a swallow.

"*De quoi avez-vous peur?*" Jeremy inquired, tilting his head as if in concern.

"I d-don't speak French," came the clearly terrified response. "Not a lick of it."

Jeremy grinned and heaved a massive sigh. "Well, that's a relief, isn't it? I was just making that up to impress you." He propped his feet up on a nearby chair and continued whittling the wood, though he had absolutely no skill in it. "What's your name, sir? This will all go much quicker if we're familiar with each other."

"Gilbert," he returned with a grunt, still eyeing the knife warily. "An' I already know who you are."

The whittling stopped and Jeremy looked at Gilbert with interest. "Do you? How disconcerting."

Gilbert finally met Jeremy's eyes. "Rook."

Jeremy blinked twice. "Bishop."

Gilbert frowned, his thick brows nearly forming into one massive expanse of hair. "What's that?"

"Are we not listing chess pieces?" Jeremy replied, giving him a surprised look. "I was preparing to get more specific with my pawns."

His impertinence did not sit well with Gilbert, who heaved a groaning sigh. "You're the Rook."

"The who?" Jeremy shook his head, pretending to be concerned. "Mr. Gilbert, you are quite incoherent. I'm nobody. Perry's the name. And I don't know what you think you know, but I can assure you," he paused and gave another quick stroke of his knife across the wood, "it isn't all that much."

"That's what you think," Gilbert said with a snort.

Jeremy stopped, and let one side of his mouth curve up into a smug, superior smile. "Excellent," he said, slowly dropping his feet from the chair and turning his body more towards Gilbert, who suddenly looked wary again. "It would be quite a shame if I were to waste my time interrogating someone who had no useful information whatsoever. I was very much hoping you would know more than I expect, because now…" He shrugged, rising smoothly and nudging his chair back with a boot.

Gilbert watched him, eyes going wider still. "N-now?" he

repeated weakly.

Again, Jeremy slid his knife down the wood, keeping his eyes on Gilbert, and dropping the newly shaved scraps into Gilbert's lap.

"Now," Jeremy told him, no longer playing at affability, "we can get somewhere."

Gilbert seemed to shrink in his seat, and Jeremy nearly smiled at the sight.

Intimidation was rather enjoyable at times.

Slowly, he began to circle Gilbert's chair, whittling away at the wood in long strokes, the sharp blade easily peeling the wood away.

"Tell me about the attack the other day. What was it you wanted? Jewels? Money? The horses?"

Gilbert said nothing, and Jeremy chuckled at the silence.

"Ah, I know, too easy." He stopped right in front of Gilbert and shaved strip after strip of wood into his lap. "Try this, then. Why, Mr. Gilbert, did you all choose Miss Dalton's carriage? I know better than to presume it was random."

"Miss who?" Gilbert asked, coughing against the sudden sawdust enveloping him.

Jeremy tapped his knife against the wood a few times, smiling again. "So, you didn't know who was within. Yet it was not random. So, you must have wanted me, then."

Gilbert swallowed, which Jeremy took to be an affirmative response.

"I'm flattered, Gilbert," he told him. "And yet you put a young lady and her companion in a dreadful sort of danger, and, as a gentleman, I find that most offensive." He slid his knife into the same hand as the wood, and slammed a right hook into Gilbert's face, the chair rocking back with the force.

He grabbed the back of it and forced it right, leaning in close. "I don't care if you wanted me or not, Gilbert," Jeremy hissed. "Attacking a coach of innocent women to get me is fouler than foul, and your precious French friends are not worth such crimes. Now, tell me why you wanted me."

"Orders," Gilbert coughed weakly, turning to spit blood onto the floor.

"From whom?" Jeremy asked, leaning closer still, the points of the knife and the wood now nearly touching Gilbert's shoulder.

"Superiors."

Jeremy let the tips press into Gilbert's shoulder just a little. "And they are...?"

Gilbert yelped but was frozen in place. "I dunno, Rook! I dunno! I jus' work for the shipping company, an' was hired wi' the rest to come inland for a while!"

"Which shipping company, I wonder?" Jeremy mused, twisting the knife and wood a little, tearing a hole in the shirt Gilbert wore.

"Cardieu's!" Gilbert winced with an audible keening sound, his left foot tapping anxiously against the floor. "Out of Bristol, Portsmouth, and Liverpool!"

Jeremy smirked and pulled back, raising a brow. "Not London, Gilbert?"

Gilbert shook his head, sighing with relief. "No, sir, Rook. Not since 1821."

Jeremy's ears began to burn, and his stomach tingled with instinctive anticipation.

1821. The year of Trace's death. At the docks. On a boat.

He cleared his throat. "Odd for a man to uproot his shipping business from the most profitable ports in England, wouldn't you agree?"

"Mr. Cardieu's interests in London failed, sir," Gilbert said, almost anxious to inform him now. "It's a small enow' operation to begin wif, and there's so much competition in London. 'E and Mr. Frank Cardieu moved offices up to Liverpool, sir, an' kept the Portsmouth and Bristol offices open, jus' in case."

"And do they prosper in Liverpool, then?" Jeremy asked, returning to whittling the wood.

"Dunno, sir. I'm a Liverpool dock worker myself, and it seems busy enough." Gilbert tried to shrug, but bound as he was, it wasn't easy. "Lots of new hires comin' and goin', just as 'e please."

Jeremy nodded slowly. "And what business would a respectable merchant such as Mr. Cardieu want with me, Gilbert?"

Gilbert's eyes widened. "Oh, 'e didn't ask for you, sir. Tha' was Mr. Mainsley, the foreman. Says we should ride out to York and wait for 'is contact, and then attack the coaches as directed."

"How many?"

"Three or four."

"And what have you taken, Gilbert?" Jeremy asked, beginning to pace around the chair again. "From these three or four coaches."

Gilbert paled at the return of Jeremy's dark tone. "J-jus' some papers, Rook. Papers and drawings from a pretty blonde, she was quite the looker…" He trailed off at Jeremy's murderous look and swallowed harshly. "Jus' papers and maps is all they asked us for. Except for you. We were s'posed to take papers an' you."

"Hmm," Jeremy mused, stroking his knife along the wood with more agitation, the tip now very sharp indeed. "Well, that's not happening, and I don't know your Mr. Mainsley, nor the Cardieus. So why, do you think, would he ask for me?"

"I dunno, Rook!" Gilbert whined. "And I dunno what that French meant 'e told us to say, it was jus' supposed to be our rally cry, you know?"

"Yes, well, unfortunately you picked the wrong rally cry." He tipped Gilbert's chair back sharply, and the man cried out again. "It's the cry of traitors, Gilbert. Traitors, murderers, thieves… French-loving reprobates who want to bring down the Crown and see France in control of the kingdom. Are you part of that effort, Gilbert? Are you a traitor to your King?"

Gilbert frantically shook his head, a sheen of perspiration dampening his skin. "N-no, Rook. No, sir. I ain't no traitor."

Jeremy hummed and rocked the chair back and forth slowly, his knife nearing Gilbert's ear. "Unfortunately, Gilbert, you are. Attacking my coach, let alone all the others, only makes you a thief. But that rally cry you were so ignorant of, and taking such poor orders from Mainsley, makes you a traitor. And there's nothing I hate more than traitors." He leaned down to his prisoner's shoulder and whispered, "Do you know what we do to traitors?"

"I ain't no traitor, Rook! I m-mean, Mr. Perry, sir," Gilbert moaned, his hands flailing in their bound state. "Honest to God, I ain't no traitor."

Jeremy tapped his knife to Gilbert's neck lightly. "Then you will have to be most accommodating, Mr. Gilbert, and answer all of my questions with complete honesty so that when I turn you over to the proper officials, I might have some evidence of your good character and loyalty. You agree?"

Gilbert nodded in jerky, panicked motions. "Yessir, yessir, I agree."

"Very good." He let the chair thump back to the floor on all four legs and moved around to the front of it. "But one thing first."

"What's tha- ARGHHH!" Gilbert broke off with a harsh shout as Jeremy shoved the sharp end of the stick into the barely-healed wound on his thigh, just as he'd done with the bayonet two days earlier.

Jeremy grabbed Gilbert's mangy hair and yanked his head close. "This is for your attack on the coach with that pretty blonde you called a looker, who happens to be like a sister to me. Had she suffered actual harm, Gilbert, this would be occurring in a place far more sensitive to you."

Gilbert whimpered, nodding as best as he could, and Jeremy yanked the wood out, eliciting another howl of pain.

"Now," Jeremy said calmly, turning away, "we can't have you taking a fever from an infected wound before I have time to turn you over, so we must clean it properly."

Gilbert groaned and panted in agony.

"Being an army man," Jeremy continued conversationally, moving to the table at one end of the room, "I know some basics of battlefield medicine." He picked up a bottle and turned back to Gilbert. "Cleansing the wound requires liquid. I've been told alcohol dulls the pain of this."

Gilbert swallowed and seemed to sigh.

Jeremy strode over and uncorked the bottle, sniffed it, then made a face. "Oh, dear. The man said it was strong stuff, but whisky has never smelled like that to me. Lord knows what it tastes like." He smirked at Gilbert. "Pity neither of us will know."

He stepped forward and poured the bottle into the wound, and Gilbert screamed, his neck straining with the pain.

"This is for the attack on my carriage," Jeremy hissed, "and for threatening, frightening, and upsetting Miss Dalton, of whom I am exceptionally fond, and for whose cause I would mete out far worse justice than this."

He lifted the bottle and stepped back, letting Gilbert moan, groan, and hiss in his chair as the wound burned with the agonies of hellfire. There was still whisky in the bottle, and Jeremy looked at it for a moment, then shrugged and downed it, shuddering as he did so.

He smacked his lips together, then gave Gilbert a disparaging look. "Definitely not what whisky should taste like. Must be local, and all whisky should be from Scotland or Ireland, right? Right." He tossed the bottle against a wall, and it shattered resoundingly.

"Now then, Gilbert," Jeremy said, wiping his hands off, "I have several more questions for you, which you are going to answer while that wound still burns so as to recall what fate awaits you if you lie. After that, I will kindly give you the closest shave you have ever had, and once you are appearing more respectable, you will favor me with 'God Save the King' in your proudest voice, all verses, three times through." He smiled and took up his chair once more, clasping his hands neatly before him. "Shall we begin?"

Helen had never understood the purpose of elaborate embroidery on one's canopy, let alone why one would have that embroidery represent a scene of a Greek tragedy or Shakespearean play.

Given that one was to sleep in their bed, and not stare up into the fabric hanging above, it seemed all too excessive.

But if one were up all night with swirling thoughts, it might be pleasant to have something to look at, and a scene such as that would surely be better than staring up at a family crest.

Even so, lying in her bed at Leighton, head throbbing, nose pounding, chest burning, she could not have wanted anything less than to see a scene of Hero and Leander hanging above her.

She coughed, sniffled, moaned, and rolled over, looking out of the window to the grounds behind Leighton, sighing the most mournful sigh of her life.

It was too cruel to catch a cold after the disaster she'd endured, but frighteningly apt. She could not have said with any real honesty that she would not have kept herself abed, or at the very least secluded in this room, without the illness, but being forced into that behavior was less than ideal.

She already felt despondent, why must she endure a further misery besides?

She closed her eyes, exhaling roughly through her mouth, as her nose was currently of no use to her.

Three days in bed, hardly able to move about her room except for the necessary things, finding less and less desire to even stir. Here in bed, she was waited on hand and foot. Her meals were all brought in on trays, she could have a fresh warming brick whenever she wanted, and endless amounts of tea. Her nieces had brought her flowers, though whether they were truly wildflowers or just weeds was unclear.

The thought was a precious one, no matter the details.

Her nephews had only brought her word of a toad, and as soon as she was well, she was to come see it.

Which, naturally, made her more inclined to remain in this warm, comfortable, toad-free bed.

Fanny was doting, but remarkably without curiosity as to the melancholy that had accompanied Helen's illness. The two were not usually connected, she was sure, and yet her most intuitive sister-in-law had said nothing on the subject. She came and read to Helen every day, doing a remarkable job with the voices, and ensured Helen never wanted for anything. It was beginning to grow rather tiresome, if not downright annoying.

Wasn't *anybody* curious as to what was going on with her? She was not a despondent sort, this was very much not like her, and yet it seemed perfectly commonplace for them. Perhaps her illness wasn't as severe as it ought to have been, but there wasn't anything to be done about that. She'd seen a physician twice now, and, short of bleeding her, which she'd refused, he had no reason to return.

Well, she was not above subjecting herself to bleeding if it came to it, but it seemed uncalled for.

Bleeding her would not bring Jeremy back.

She sighed again, this time with a heaviness to her heart.

Jeremy.

She'd seen his face in her mind's eye a hundred times, if not more, while she'd laid here with nothing to do, dozing fitfully. His smile, his laugh, the mischievous twinkle in his eye, even the horrid disguise he'd worn at first. All made her smile, then weep, and then smile again.

Mr. Pratt the fop. Mr. Perry the ruffian. Jeremy the tease. She loved all of them, all of *him*, and yet he had let her go. He had abandoned her to her family as though she had been no more than a charge to him.

As though it really had been just an assignment.

Surely that could not be true. Surely he had been honest with her when he'd told her of his feelings, his sincerity, and when they had kissed…

Surely that had all been real.

But there was no way to know, she supposed. He had acted a part for her before, why should he not again?

Was she a fool for believing him? Or had that been truth, and he'd turned coward when it became too much?

She winced and buried her face in the mattress. Now she was growing even more dramatic and fanciful. Jeremy Pratt was anything but a coward, as his actions during the attack had proven. If he had left her behind, and what he had said to her was true, as she had to believe, then she could only presume that he was doing so because he felt it was right.

Because he had to.

But why should he have to? Had she said or done something to suddenly make a romance between them impossible or unwise? Had the attack somehow changed his mind?

Too many questions, not enough answers, and no way to change that. She had no idea where he had gone after he'd left here, and she could not ask the one person who knew Jeremy Pratt had seen her to York.

Rafe would kill Jeremy if he had any idea that he and Helen had shared anything resembling a romantic encounter when unaccompanied, especially if Rafe had been the one to bring Jeremy on.

But Rafe could also tell her more about Jeremy, as he knew the real Jeremy and not the version everybody else did.

Or she could write to Mr. John Pratt, and see if he might be more forthcoming about his brother's whereabouts and intentions, but that seemed somehow even more farfetched. Jeremy had said that his brother was reserved, and the questions she would ask would be of a rather personal nature.

Jeremy had said once that he had to be sure of himself as no one else was, and she, so headstrong and caught up in the moment, had said that she was. At that moment, she had been.

But was she now?

What should she believe? What *could* she believe? Jeremy had been so many people, so many versions, and there hadn't been time enough to be certain of anything but her own inclination, and there wasn't much to recommend that to anyone in any regard.

Helen was as human and fanciful as any girl in the world, no matter what she would have claimed, and Jeremy Pratt had turned her completely silly.

She rolled to her back and stared up at Hero and Leander, clearly miserable without each other, though not yet dead from their extreme longings.

Helen could relate to that sentiment, but she wondered if Jeremy would. Longing for her love, wishing he could brave the dangers to be with her, fearing what would become of her without him... Poor Hero. Helen had never felt much sympathy for her before, nor any of the romantic heroines with tragic tales to tell, but now she felt a strange kinship with the damsels.

Lord, what would Margaret and Rosalind say if they knew how maudlin Helen had grown? Rosalind might not even recognize it, as she was blissfully engaged in her new marriage and sailing off to adventures elsewhere with the man of her dreams. She was the victorious heroine whose resistance had given way at last, and her dashing hero had swept her off her feet.

Margaret had her hero, too, and made the most of it. Happily ever after was her reality, as her young daughter and impending second child indicated, and her eyes needed no sight but that of her adoring husband.

Yet another man who was more than he appeared.

By all accounts, it was Helen's turn. By rights, this should have worked in her favor. But here she was, without a man, without love, and without hope.

What a perfectly dismal thought.

She would be a spinster. An eternal spinster who had known a grand total of thirty-six hours of love, if that, and no more. Never expressed out loud, never truly fathomed beyond her own acknowledgment of the sensation. No proof that it existed in any way beyond the memory.

Never more than a memory.

Her friends had reality. She had memory.

Stop comparing yourself with anybody else, Helen, love. You're not like any other person in this world, let alone any woman, or any of your friends. But I'll be damned if that means there is anything at all lacking in a single part of you.

Helen whimpered and closed her eyes as Jeremy's voice resonated in her mind, just as strong and fervent as it had been the day he had said it. It ought to have pained her to hear it, but she took strength and comfort from it instead. She felt her heart warm, and it had nothing to do with sickness.

Jeremy would have healed her. His smile, his laughter, his deprecating humor, his incessant teasing, all would have sunk into her with more efficacy and nourishment than anything a doctor could give her. One kick to her shins, and she would have been up and out of this bed and waltzing about the house.

But he was not here, only in her memories.

So, she would take that and run with it.

If Jeremy Pratt had loved her, did love her, or had any chance of loving her in the future, she had to be a woman worthy of the love of Jeremy Pratt. A woman he *could* love. A woman who could match him in vitality, effort, and substance.

Not this weak and simpering creature lying in her bed bemoaning her state.

She was Helen Elizabeth Dalton, and she was better than this. She could be the woman Jeremy deserved. The woman she would want the man she loved to be married to. The woman he would not wish to live without.

The woman he would swim the Hellespont for.

Helen grinned and nodded to herself, sitting up and swinging her legs over the edge of the bed.

A wave of dizziness swept over her and her head pounded furiously.

Right. Illness.

She moaned and fell back down to the pillows, though her feet still hung off the bed, and she swung them in a half-hearted attempt to take on the energy she was feeling, though her body was not yet strong enough to endure it.

But it would be. She would take the broth, and the baths, and the tea, and she would let her body heal. Then she would find the strength to be herself, with all the faults and failings she'd ever had, but with a renewed sense of who she was and what she wanted. She would clear her mind of the clouds, gloom, and despair and find a way to smile and laugh.

Or, at the very least, refrain from crying so much.

Even now, her eyes filled with tears, and her will weakened.

Poor, pitiful, pathetic Helen, sick in bed and missing a man who might not miss her.

She had to believe he missed her. She *had* to.

Or else she couldn't believe a single word he'd said, and she couldn't bear that. She would never be able to trust again if he'd been false to her, and she could not go through life being suspicious, cynical, and cold.

No, Jeremy had meant it, every word, she was sure of it.

And the moment she had any indication he was ready to act as such and take her on, she would be ready for him.

But for the moment, she was still ill. He was still gone. And it still hurt.

So, she could cry the welling tears without rebuke.

Just this once.

Chapter Eleven

"All this time and no one thought to clean the place?" Jeremy snorted and looked around, rubbing at the back of his head. "If Trace isn't dead, he'd wish he was the moment he set foot in here."

He shuddered, looking around the filthy, dark, mostly-in-shambles entryway of Parkerton Lodge, wondering what in the world he was doing here.

Of course, he knew very well what he was doing here, he'd been assigned to come here and find something. Not anything specific, just something.

Parkerton Lodge had been turned over and practically destroyed in the attempts to find whatever something they seemed to think Trace had left behind, every secret unearthed from top to bottom by members of the Foreign Office, Home Office, War Office, and even the Convent contingent, not to mention Trace's brothers in the League. All of them had tried to find something.

The best covert operatives and investigators England had to offer, and he was supposed to find something they all missed?

Not bloody likely.

But from the state of things, it had been quite some time since anybody had looked for anything in this place, except perhaps for animals seeking shelter. The tapestries had mostly been torn down, now riddled with dust and moth, and in some cases eaten away. The gilded ceilings were faded and strewn with cobwebs, stained from water and crumbling in places. The wallpaper peeled, cracked, and had some mysterious stains that Jeremy had no desire to investigate. Furniture was overturned and broken, sheets that had once covered paintings and fabrics were now strewn on the filthy floor, and at least half of the paintings had either been taken down or stolen, but shadows of their placement remained on the walls that had borne them.

Jeremy's footsteps echoed eerily in the house, though without the crispness they should have done, had the debris and grime beneath him not muffled the sound. He said nothing more aloud, even in jest, for there was something disconcerting about being in a place like this. Haunting, really. The master of this house had died a violent death that had yet to be avenged or understood, and yet something must have felt off about that, if the Shopkeepers, or at the very least Tailor and Weaver, thought there was a chance he was alive.

This house had nothing within it to indicate its master might not have met his death that night on the docks. It had been abandoned all that time, the servants shuttled off to other employment, the estate never sold or razed. It was curious indeed, considering Trace's death. But then, it would not have surprised Jeremy one iota if the League, or the Shopkeepers, or one of the national offices had some ownership or authority where their operatives' holdings were concerned.

Still, he doubted he would find anything new in this place, he thought as he wandered each and every room, his eye scouring the place for details. Everything was faded, as though whatever life had existed here was some distant memory, and whatever secrets had been in place no longer could be.

The sideboards had all been stripped of doors and drawers. The once-stately desk in the study was overturned, a secret compartment exposed, and two drawers on the floor beside it. All throughout the halls, random floorboards were ripped up, exposing nothing but the structural work beneath. Every single bedroom had been overturned, and the master's chambers were in utter shambles.

Amateurs. As if an operative of Trace's caliber would have kept his most important documents and information in such obvious hiding places.

Surely, they ought to have known that.

But it was clear from the complete abandon with which they had taken on the investigation that no one who had truly understood

Trace as a man or an operative had been involved. Or if they had, there was no evidence of it left behind.

Jeremy had met Trace once before, back when he was being recruited for covert operations. Trace had been just a few years older, though he had seemed decades beyond him. He had been a very intense sort of man, his eyes holding a depth and gravity to them that spoke of a hard life, or perhaps that he had seen too much, and yet there was nothing remotely resembling fatigue in his features or his manner.

He was always alert, and the fleeting interaction had left an indelible impression on Jeremy.

In a way, he was honored to have taken his place, though the reason for it was disturbing, and he was honored now to be trusted with finding the truth, though he felt fairly unworthy to do so.

He exhaled now, having made a cursory study of the entire house. "All right, Trace. Tell me where to go."

He thought back over the place from top to bottom, room by room, putting everything back the way it must have been when it was inhabited.

Trace hadn't entertained much, from what he understood from Weaver, who had given Jeremy every file they had on him. He had been a reserved man, though hardly stoic. He'd always taken the most dangerous assignments and completed them with unusual thoroughness. He could inhabit the darkest realms without anyone suspecting him, and yet he'd been well thought of by his local associates. Never quite part of the upper crust, but an orphan with minimal fortune and prospects would endure that.

When his uncle and guardian, Lord Parkerton, had officially named him heir, the tide of opinion shifted more in the favor of Alexander Sommerville, but by then, his ways and nature had been set.

He'd not cared for the opinions of others, nor had he seen himself as above or below anyone. He'd been a committed soldier, a capable landowner and master, and a damned good operative. The best that they had ever seen, Weaver had told Jeremy. His loss had been felt throughout the entire chain of command in England, though it could never be acknowledged publicly.

But then, his death had not been, either.

No funeral, no memorial service, no corpse to bury.

Only one person outside of the ranks had been informed of the loss.

Miss Poppy Edgewood.

And even that had rankled some.

From what Jeremy understood, Miss Edgewood had been informed that her intended had died at sea, and, as is customary, he had been buried there. The lie was easy to tell, easier to live, because they had no proof otherwise.

But the League had felt bound to Miss Edgewood from that day on, given the sincere and apparently quite profound attachment between Trace and herself, and so to this day, she was watched over by no less than three contacts of theirs up here in Cheshire. Every other month or so, one of the League members would travel up to Cheshire and "tend the flowers," which had been the phrase intimated in the last will and testament, according to Rogue, who happened to be Trace's cousin and the only family member of significance.

What exactly that had meant had been a little less clear, but there was no doubt Trace had meant for them all to mind the woman he loved and had left behind without ties to bind her to his estate, fortune, or impending title.

So, they had kept her well-guarded, ensured her safety at all times, and occasionally provided her with additional funds by inconspicuous means. Not that she was aware of their intervention in any way, just as she had never been informed of the true nature of what her late intended had been involved in.

Poppy Edgewood would not recognize a single one of them if they had knocked on her door, and nor would she be in any way useful to their enemy.

Even so, she was now the responsibility of the League, in honor of Trace.

Jeremy looked around the house with a new perspective, something tingling in the back of his mind. If Trace was as devoted to Miss Edgewood as he'd been led to believe, she might have been in this house several times. According to the file, she was a clever woman, bright and lively, and surely would have noticed if Trace had behaved in any way suspicious. She might have even been able to weed out a hiding place, if her curiosity had been piqued enough to look for one.

If she were anything at all like Helen, she most certainly would have tried.

Helen...

Jeremy jerked his attention away from the all-too-tempting thoughts of her and forced himself to focus on the house.

He looked up at the grand staircase, now a rather poor imitation of its former days. The dark wood of the railing and its spindles, now a musty grey from its coating of dust, would have once glinted and shone with a well-polished finish in the candlelight. Given the number of sconces on the wall, that light would have been abundant. The stairs themselves were of the same dark wood, and while several parts were warped and splintering, they would have been smooth and polished, perfect for Helen to have made a grand entrance before they set off to attend a ball or other social occasion.

She would have been loveliness itself no matter what she had chosen from her wardrobe, which he had to presume was extensive, given the sheer volume of luggage she had travelled to York with. He wouldn't care what she wore, only that she was his.

Frowning, he shook his head quickly, striding up the stairs back towards the bedrooms, wondering faintly if the pained creaking of those stairs could indicate some structural instability.

There would have been too much irony in falling to his death in Trace's house.

While thinking of Helen.

He *had* to be focused. He had to think of Trace, of the investigation, of unearthing something that could help them win this bloody fight that no one else knew about.

The master bedchamber gave him nothing to go off of on his second pass, but he hadn't expected it to. He doubted that Trace would have hidden his notes in the bureau or under the mattress of his bed, no matter how other operatives seemed to think he might. He turned the mattress back over, coughing slightly when the dust kicked up in a fury, and sank down onto its filthy surface.

Clothing was still in the bureau, though none of it was neat or tidy anymore. Trace's clothing. As though he ought to have just shortly returned from London and taken up his comfortable and quiet existence in the country.

Jeremy smiled a little at that. Country living or not, there was nothing ever quiet or comfortable about their lifestyle. Cap lived in the country with his family when not in London, and the Faction had found them there. There was always a plot to mull over, some case that needed consideration, some danger hanging over their heads.

It was thrilling to be part of, and Jeremy, for one, loved the constant state of activity it gave him.

But at the moment...

Had Trace had reservations about his assignments, given the future he had planned for himself and Miss Edgewood? He'd never refused an assignment, as far as the records indicated, and had, at times, volunteered for the riskiest ones. But had he feared the outcomes? Had he been hesitant to take anything up?

Had love made him question it all?

Jeremy, as the Rook, had no ties to concern him. He'd never hesitated, questioned, worried, or balked in any way at what was being asked of him. His life was given up in the service of the Crown freely, and he'd never been concerned about that.

But now...

He saw Helen everywhere, in everything, and thought of her constantly. Even in a rundown, turned over, abandoned place like this, he saw her. The ballroom would have been her favorite room, and he had spent too long imagining her waltzing about on her own to tease him about the lack of opportunities she had to dance. The music room had her walking the perimeter with a scowl on her face, poking him about the state of things, then laughing at the demolished pianoforte, finding it rather perfect for her talents.

This wasn't even his house, for pity's sake! He shouldn't be imagining Helen anywhere in here. He was supposed to be focusing on Trace and the mysteries his death had left them all enshrouded in.

But knowing about Miss Edgewood, and Trace's feelings for her, made Helen more a part of this than Jeremy could have imagined.

It was interfering with everything.

Yet he had never been more grateful.

He hesitated now with the thought of plunging headlong into danger and violence, though there was no understanding between them. He could not see how he could give himself up with the same fervor to his work, his missions, knowing what he would leave behind.

Had his late colleague felt the same? Did his current colleagues feel similarly?

Yet they pressed forward just as they had always done, without much by way of turbulence and no hint of reluctance.

It did not seem possible at the moment.

But his own emotions and confusion could not interfere now. He had done what was best by seeing Helen safe and secure with her family, and then pressing forward with the investigation. He had seen Mr. Gilbert properly interrogated, though perhaps with a bit more of a personal sentiment than the Rook had usually taken up with the process, which would undoubtedly make its way into the report to Weaver. No matter, as Weaver tended to enjoy the variation to interrogation, but it would raise questions. The contacts had seen Gilbert back to London for his fate, and off to Cheshire Jeremy had gone.

He'd not admitted his feelings to Helen or given her any reason to think of him in any particular way. She was safe from the danger of his life, and that was what mattered.

Had Miss Edgewood been similarly kept safe from Trace's life?

If she had, and if she had ever been a regular guest at Parkerton, there was no way in hell that he would have kept compromising evidence within its walls, especially if she were to become his wife.

He might have risked his own life, but he would never have risked hers.

In the event that his identity had been compromised, he wouldn't have stashed anything in the house to further complicate matters. Certainly nothing to make his loved ones in any way part of the danger. Nothing...

Jeremy's eyes widened and he stilled, though he hadn't exactly been moving. Nothing in the house.

He wouldn't have left anything in the house.

They would have found it by now if he had, and it was too obvious for a careful operative like Trace. His assignments might have been risky, but he never had been with himself or anything else. He was thorough, detailed, prepared, and that innate alertness in him kept him safe in every dangerous venture, apart from the last.

No, he would never have left it here. He was not a man to sit within a house that may never have been a home for him, poring over documents in a study like a landowner might do with ledgers.

Trace was active and engaged.

And madly in love.

Jeremy felt a new and sudden kinship with his fallen comrade, and before he knew what he was about, he was flying back down the rickety stairs, ignoring the peeling paper, dusty tapestries, and general disarray. He pushed open a glass-paned door, though the glass was nearly all broken or cracked, and moved out onto the terrace, overgrown with wisteria and ivy. He barely saw any of that; he was more concerned with the gardens and lands.

All overgrown and wild, but something told him he was on the right path.

He skimmed through the notes in his head, reminding himself what he knew. The house and lands were part of the Parkerton title, but the lands were not particularly expansive. They did, however, neighbor a very pretty estate known as Whitesdown, where the Edgewood family lived. They were undoubtedly the predominant family in the area, aside from Lord Parkerton, but the orphaned son of Parkerton's unfortunate brother would not have been a prospect for such a family's eldest daughter, until he'd been named heir.

But before then, he'd simply been an unsuitable suitor, which seemed to have been precisely what Poppy Edgewood liked.

Young lovers across these lands? The rolling hills and breeze swept grasses, dotted with wildflowers and magnificent trees, would have been all too picturesque, and exactly what they would wish for themselves.

Helen would love this place, and he would have loved to have her here. Running across the lands, exploring with all the eagerness of a child, laughing gaily through the fields, that long, blonde hair billowing out behind her…

He would have followed her to the ends of the earth for such a chance, such a look. He would have spent every waking moment with her, had she been his neighbor. Had they grown up together, she would already have been his. He would never have let her escape, never given her up, never left her without ensuring she knew exactly how he felt.

Every moment would be...

Precious.

Jeremy stopped his wandering of the gardens, much of which had been overturned with shovels or spades, and stared off in the distance, eyeing Whitesdown.

He put the imposing and terrifying image of Trace out of his mind and concentrated on the much more human and relatable Alex Sommerville. He had a girl he loved and knew his time with her was not to be wasted.

He'd never sit around in his own house, on his own lands, letting his work get in the way of time with her, just as he would never have kept incriminating or dangerous evidence in a place easily discovered.

And yet, he was not the sort to go waltzing into Whitesdown when her family did not approve.

"So where did you go, Alex, hmm?" Jeremy mused aloud, clasping his hands behind him as he strode away from the garden at Parkerton. "You want to see your girl as often as you can, you need to retrieve information or go over it, provided you hadn't memorized it, or you need to put new things away... You're not wasteful, you make the most of everything, so..."

He trailed off, walking towards Whitesdown carefully, knowing the Edgewoods had long since given up the house and gone off to Derbyshire, though Poppy had remained on a farm just outside of the village. Cast off by the family, ridiculed by those of her class, and suspected of behavior not becoming of a young lady, due to her abject mourning.

Regardless, someone else lived in Whitesdown, and they would not take kindly to a stranger coming to see their house and look for secrets within its walls or on its grounds.

Alex would never have done that, so it must have been something else. Something sentimental, yet convenient. Something that would never raise suspicions or seem at all conspicuous.

One mile to Whitesdown, perhaps more, but the hills were such that it could be seen clearly from the south-facing windows of Parkerton, and from the lands. It was a pretty place; the sort that a man from Alex's background would have found epitomizing all that was unattainable. And yet there would have been the bright, gleaming figure of Poppy Edgewood to bring it down to his level.

He would have done everything to avoid Whitesdown itself.

But surely between the lands, where things were less defined...

Jeremy turned a little to the right, veering west, strolling along as easily as a simple man might do in such countryside, and dressed as he was, no one would have pegged him for a wealthy gentleman. Which was well, as he was suddenly fixated on a very familiar-looking farm in the distance. Odd that he'd never made the connection when he was "tending the flowers," but she could see the shadows of Parkerton Lodge from her lowly farmhouse.

Yet not Whitesdown.

Significant, he thought. Not particularly useful at the moment, but significant.

He'd have to remember that when...

His thought would remain unfinished, as a rather large oak with rather perfect climbing branches was suddenly before him, almost squarely between Whitesdown and Parkerton. But it was not the branches, nor its position, that made the tree intriguing.

It was the bench beneath it.

From a distance, it appeared completely usual, and fairly common by construction and style. It was an odd placement for a bench, certainly, considering the distance from either estate, or any other dwelling. And the scenery, while admirable, wasn't any more picturesque than anything else around him, and perhaps even less so.

No reason at all for this bench to be here, fine tree or not.

Jeremy approached both, his senses on alert, his mind whirling. He circled the tree, eyeing it up and down, and, though he highly doubted it would help, he knocked on the trunk. Sure enough, it was solid.

He smiled to himself. "Too easy, Trace, I know."

He paused as he caught sight of a rough heart carved into the bark, and the letters A and P carved in the middle of it.

"Very romantic, Alex," Jeremy praised, nodding to himself. "I'm sure Poppy loved that."

It was a surprisingly sentimental thing, actually, and no relation of Rogue could ever be sentimental. It was too much a stretch, and while Trace had been hailed as the more congenial of the pair, that hardly indicated that he was truly a congenial fellow. Jeremy, for one, found the word a trifle generous for anyone in that family, except, perhaps, for Lady Geraldine.

This tree wasn't anything special, apart from the romantic carving, so Jeremy turned to the bench itself.

What struck him was how very boring a bench it was. For a sentimental man who carved on the tree, the bench was remarkably unadorned. No carvings of any kind, no initials, no hearts, not even worn places from hours of sitting.

Yet the grass around it was worn enough, and some from recent use. A small bouquet of wildflowers lay to one side of it, and Jeremy avoided them as he would have a headstone in a cemetery.

He circled the bench once, twice, and then stopped, staring at the seat of it.

That was rather thick, unless they expected elephants to sit on it.

Unless Miss Edgewood's parents were related to a species of water buffalo, that was unnecessary.

Jeremy moved to the bench, looking at the seat with interest. Was it a drawer? Did the planks come loose? Or was the bench a diversion for some rather large rock nearby?

It couldn't be obvious, or Poppy would have discovered it. So perhaps...

He shook the first plank, then the second, and third...

A soft click met his ears, and he grinned to himself. "Conniving and romantic, Alex. Good man."

The plank pried off easily, and the one next to it, though it would appear it was unable to be pried off first. The mechanism wasn't particularly important, though he would have to set it all back when he was done. Poppy must be protected, after all, and if this was a frequent place for her patronage, he'd leave it undisturbed.

No sense in uprooting her peace just because her late intended had secrets.

All told, three planks were removed on one side, and two on the other, given the varied width of the planks. Beneath them was another stretch of wood, though it seemed to be thinner. It wasn't obvious from the sides, and nor was it obvious beneath.

"Come on, Trace," Jeremy muttered. "How'd you do this without making a ruddy scene?"

He felt around the edges, then lifted a little, and the whole thing hinged up towards him like the lid to a chest. He knelt before the bench and peered inside, his eyes widening.

Papers and files, illustrations in Hal's hand, missives in Weaver's hand, the untidy scrawl of Rogue on scraps and notes...

He shoved aside the familiar things, then his eyes widened further.

A lifetime of work was beneath it all, and it would take months to analyze everything, if not years.

"Oh, saints preserve us," Jeremy breathed in a perfect imitation of his Irish mother's brother Patrick. He looked up to the sky, though he had never been a religious man. "Trace, you damned genius, I hate you."

He looked up at the face of the bench then, and saw, for the first time, a single solitary carving. Very small, very faint, but it was there.

A poppy.

Jeremy exhaled roughly, shaking his head. "Romantic, conniving, genius... Bloody hell."

Now they could get somewhere.

Chapter Twelve

The peculiar thing about hope is that something somewhere has to feed it for it to live on.

Helen didn't have that.

She had nothing, as it happened.

She'd lost count of how many days she'd been at Leighton now. How many mornings she had woken up in the same bed after having dreams of Jeremy. How many smiles she'd had to force for her brother, sister-in-law, nieces, and nephews.

How many tears she'd hidden.

It all seemed rather pathetic and dramatic when she thought about it too much. Why should she be agonizing so much over something that had no name? She'd flirted shamelessly with a man, then she'd gone for a coach ride with him as her protector, and then, God help her, she'd fallen in love with him.

She'd fallen in love with a man, and he'd saved her life, then dropped her at her brother's estate like a disobedient child.

Of course, she hadn't told him she'd been foolish enough to love him, which had undoubtedly saved her a good deal of pain. If he'd known about her feelings and still dropped her off without a word, she would have been heartbroken and felt as though the world had dropped from under her feet.

Now she only felt foolish.

So, so foolish. She kicked at a tree in agitation, only for the soft material of her slippers to bend easily against the bark, causing swift and sudden pain to flare in two of her toes.

Perhaps three.

She winced and gripped at them tightly, groaning through gritted teeth, then lowered her foot to the ground slowly, exhaling.

She was a fool, and now she had the injury to prove it.

"Walking the grounds again, Helen? You're not a walker, so it must be a serious issue."

Helen stopped as the most familiar voice in the world teased her.

The most familiar, but not the one she wanted.

"How do you know I have walked the grounds so much, Mother?" Helen asked, not turning around. "You've been here, what, ten minutes?"

"Seven, to be precise," her mother replied, not sounding any closer.

Helen groaned, folding her arms. "Why must you always do that? Why do you always have to make light of everything?"

"I'm not making light, love. It's really been seven minutes." She heard her mother's footsteps then, and Helen steeled herself. "I entered the house, kissed Charles and Fanny, asked after you, and Fanny told me everything. And I came straight out to you."

"I am perfectly all right, Mother," Helen ground out, her eyes beginning to well up.

Her mother hummed a disbelieving noise, and then her hand was on Helen's arm. "You never call me 'Mother', my lamb. You're not all right, are you?"

Now the tears came with full force, and Helen shook her head, swallowing repeatedly. "No, Mama. Not even a little bit."

She was suddenly turned and pulled into a tight embrace, the sort that only a mother could give. And Josephine Dalton was exceptionally good at it. Helen crumpled against her, burying her face as her mother's hands ran down her hair and made soothing circles on her back.

Though she had cried for days, though she had thought herself beyond sobbing, everything came rushing back while in her mother's arms, and she suddenly found herself unable to stop crying. Wounds she had thought healed opened up, still raw and burning, and through it all, she felt embarrassed beyond belief.

To feel so much for a man who might not return any of the sentiments? It was beyond anything. How could she have let herself believe so easily? How could she have been so foolish, so naïve, and so completely without sense?

To love a man so filled with secrets. A man who could become anyone or anything, behave however it suited him for the task at hand.

He could have lied to her in the coach, could have said whatever he wanted to make her believe him. That was what he did, and even if Rafe… If Rafe…

Rafe made Jeremy accompany her. Rafe was the same sort of man. He became who he had to, and yet Margaret loved him. Trusted him. Knew him.

But how could she be sure?

How could Helen?

"Come on, lamb, your brother is watching," her mother soothed as she pulled back. "He's a terrible snoop, and he'll be watching from the window."

Helen laughed a watery laugh and wiped at her eyes. "He hasn't asked a single question, not even one. It has to be eating away at him."

Her mother chuckled, her eyes crinkling at the corners, just as Helen's did. "Oh, undoubtedly. Poor Charles has always been a curious lad. Polite, but curious." She linked her arm with Helen's and started walking with her around the garden, rubbing her arm. "Do you want to tell me what's troubling you?"

Helen sighed, folding her arms tightly across her faded green muslin. "Not really, Mama. There's more to it than just being attacked by highwaymen."

Her mother made a loud scoffing sound that surprised Helen. "Oh, I know that, Helen. You were involved in a break in and robbery at Margaret's home, and you slept through the night straightaway. You're no simpering miss, a bit of danger isn't going to turn you inside out and upside down like this."

That was unexpected, and Helen looked at her mother in surprise. "How did you know I slept through the night?"

Her mother returned her look with a nearly identical one of her own. "Did you think I wouldn't check in on you after something like that? I missed that first night only because you insisted on staying with Margaret, and I had you looked in on."

Helen laughed once, shaking her head. "You are such a devious woman."

Her mother smirked, keeping her strides long and even as she walked with Helen. "Surely this is not the first time you have come to that conclusion?"

No, it was not, but it seemed that every time she was reminded of it, the reality of it doubled. She was always surprised by her mother, whether it was her humor, her intuition, or some new discovery.

Helen shook her head and leaned on her mother a little, finding solace in her presence that she hadn't known she'd been missing. Or needing.

She'd been so wrapped up in missing Jeremy, battling between believing him and not believing him, that she'd not even realized how lonely she'd been. She would have loved to have chatted with Rosalind, and rage about men and their foibles with her, only Rosalind was off on the sea with the man she only now realized she was madly in love with.

Margaret would have been a better choice, given the ties between her husband and Jeremy, and Margaret would understand being driven mad by a man with secrets. But Margaret was expecting and thus delicate, and her husband was the most overprotective man on the planet, not to mention that the road she would have to take to get there had highwaymen, as Helen could attest to.

As universally liked as Helen seemed to be, she really didn't have many other friends.

But there was her mother.

"Come over here, lamb," her mother said, indicating a stone bench. "Come sit and talk with me."

Helen shook her head with a sigh. "I've done nothing but sit, or lie, for days, Mama. Weeks. I had a cold that would not go away, and no desire to get up as it was."

"Hmm," her mother murmured, strangely not sounding at all disapproving. "You've always enjoyed life, even when you were cranky or furious. You hate being idle. What could possibly keep you in bed with no desire to leave it, cold or no cold?"

There was a strong tone to her mother's words, a rather knowing one, and Helen suspected she already knew the answer.

But not the details.

"You're not going to stop until I tell you, are you?" Helen asked with a sigh.

"I am not," her mother confirmed with a nod. "And what's worse, I'll put Tibby on you as well."

Helen shuddered at the suggestion but knowing better than to doubt it. There was a longstanding friendship between her mother and Lady Raeburn, undoubtedly the most terrifying woman on the planet, and one of the most lovable. When one was not finding her interfering beyond reckoning.

"I am not sure what I can tell you, Mama," Helen admitted, looking down at the wilting rose bushes on the path. "There are secrets… Secrets I don't understand, and they're not mine to tell."

"I am glad to hear it," her mother praised, her voice fairly mellow for the topic. "I never trust a person who has no secrets. Nor do I want to know these secrets, if they are not yours. Tell me what you can, leave out what you must."

Helen stared at her in disbelief. "You're going to stand there and say that. You?"

For the first time, her mother looked at her severely. "Yes, I am, although I am walking, not standing. I want to know your secrets, lamb, like any mother does, but I don't want to know anybody else's." Then she smiled a little, and a familiar twinkle appeared in her eyes. "Unless it happens to be particularly good gossip, and then I am all ears."

"Oh, Mother…" Helen scoffed, rolling her eyes.

"You didn't think Tibby was alone in her gossip-loving ways, did you?" her mother asked with a nudge. Then she sobered and adjusted her cream shawl over her calico gown. "I want you to feel as though you can talk to me about anything, Helen. Even this."

Helen nodded slowly, and exhaled, taking quite a long time to do so. "I was escorted here by a man Marlowe brought in. You know that part, but what you don't know is… he was a man I knew back in London."

"No…"

"A man," Helen continued, ignoring her mother's gasp, "of whom I had become particularly fond. I didn't know that he would be there, and I don't believe Rafe knew I had feelings for this man. Nor, I think, did he suspect that this man might have had... feelings for me. Rafe wouldn't have allowed it, you know how protective he is, and I can't even be sure that the man did have feelings for me, though he claimed..."

Her mother covered Helen's hands, squeezing gently. "Shush, lamb, you're talking yourself in circles. What happened?"

Helen hiccupped a weak sob. "I fell in love with him, Mama. I got to know him on this journey, who he really is, beneath everything I thought I knew in London, and that man..." She exhaled roughly and blinked up at the grey skies, desperate to clear the wash of tears.

"Oh, lamb..." her mother almost whimpered, rubbing her arm.

She sniffed and shook her head. "I loved that man, Mama. And I thought he might have... He led me to believe... But he had secrets, so many secrets, and I don't know..."

"Stop right there," her mother interrupted quietly. "Stop now."

Helen clamped down on her lips and rubbed her fingers together.

Her mother turned and waited for Helen to meet her gaze. Only when their eyes met, did she speak again. "Why, if you felt that way, do you now speak of it in the past tense?"

"Pardon?"

Her mother smiled a little. "You said you loved that man. Loved. Not love."

"Oh, Mama," Helen groaned, taking a step away. "Particulars?"

"Times like these," her mother sighed, "particulars are the most important. So. Do you still love this man?"

Helen tipped her head back as though there was a beam of sunlight to warm her skin. "Yes."

Memories she had been pushing away, had thought too painful to recall, sprang back to life. Jeremy, leaning against the corner of the coach as it rolled on, watching her with a smile as she talked. The two of them together in the driver's seat, laughing uproariously about something or other, not caring if they were heard. The feeling of anticipation before his foot crossed her shins, and the exhilaration when it did.

That night when she'd kissed him, and they'd sat on opposite sides of the door, fingers touching beneath it.

The impossible hope she had felt when he had kissed her the next morning.

"Yes, I love him," Helen said again, opening her eyes and staring at her mother steadily. She shrugged her shoulders, smiling sadly. "But after the attack, he barely spoke to me again. We pushed on through the night, in the pouring rain, and did not stop until we arrived here. And then he only said a handful of words to me, all politeness. And then he left."

"Ah…" her mother said softly.

Helen glared at her, wondering how her mother could react without the same indignation burning through her at being dumped here. "What does that mean? What sort of a reaction is that?"

Her mother shrugged and started to walk again, and Helen had no choice but to follow her. "I was just wondering what bothers you more, love; the fact that he has secrets or the fact that he left you here?"

"Why does it have to be one or the other?" Helen demanded. "Both of them bother me."

"No, love," her mother said with a smile. "They don't. One feeds the other. Which is it?"

A cold chill sank into the pit of Helen's stomach, and she stared at her mother for quite a long moment.

Which was worse? Not knowing his secrets, or being left by him?

"He left me here," Helen admitted in a small voice. "He just… left. Without a word to me about if he were coming back, about if he would write, about how he felt… As though I meant nothing and that what we had shared…"

"What exactly *had* you shared, Helen?" her mother asked sharply, as only a mother could.

Helen smirked at the implication. "Nothing I couldn't tell you, Mama, but I don't see the point. It all meant nothing to him, clearly."

Her mother made a face of consideration, then shook her head. "I doubt that, but I could be wrong."

"I doubt everything," Helen muttered, shaking her head. "Everything he said, and everything he did, and my own feelings…"

"Why those?" her mother asked. "Your feelings are the truest thing, why doubt them?"

"Because he doesn't return them!" Helen cried. "How could he return them and just leave me here? Without a word, without a kiss, without anything at all? We were so close to it, Mama, just inches away from happiness, and then that damned attack happened…"

"Where he saved your life, and everyone else's, pushed on despite being injured, and drove straight through the night in the pouring rain just to see you safely delivered and out of harm's way." Her mother lifted a brow with an imperious tilt.

Helen frowned, sensing her argument had just been neatly turned upside down. "Yes, what of it? He was hired to do so. He wanted to see the task done."

Her mother smiled at her, somehow amused despite everything. "Oh, was he hired? I thought Marlowe just brought him in. If you knew him in London, he must be some sort of gentleman, and a man like that wouldn't be hired on for such a thing. Did he say he was being paid for it?"

"No," Helen grumbled, "but it was an assignment."

"But he knew it was going to be you," her mother pressed. "Marlowe told him your identity, yes?"

She'd never thought of that, but she supposed he must have. "So it would seem."

"And if you were fond of him, he had to at least pretend to be fond of you, and to then go with you from London to York, just because Marlowe asked it of him…" Her mother hummed again, then looked at Helen, still smirking. "Did he do anything untoward?"

"Mother!" Helen screeched, her cheeks heating. "No, for heaven's sake! Jeremy is a gentleman in every way, and he never once attempted anything improper!"

Her mother grinned swiftly. "Ah, not opportunistic, then. So, he, being fond of you, or at least pretending, behaved with respect and honor all the way to York."

Helen scowled at that. "Yes, he did, and you needn't be so superior about it."

"Oh, but I will be, lamb," her mother replied, shaking her head. "I will. This man you love didn't drop you here to get rid of you. Don't you see? He was charged with protecting you, and he failed."

"Oh, don't be ridiculous," Helen spat, striding off in agitation. "We were attacked, it is not as though he arranged it. He was splendid, absolutely marvelous, heroic, and dashing… And all that I wanted was for him to sweep me into his arms and hold me tightly. But then he packed me into the carriage and brought me straight here."

Her mother laughed under her breath. "But he did fail, lamb. He was to keep you safe, and he did not. How could he face you after that? He clearly felt responsible for you, as he should have, and you had nearly come to harm."

"No!" Helen insisted. "No…"

"It's unforgivable, really," she went on. "He only had to do one thing, and he couldn't manage it."

"Mama, stop!" Helen pleaded. "He fought off at least five men, nearly single-handedly, and drove straight on through the night without sleep! In the rain, Mama!"

Her mother rolled her eyes dramatically. "Oh, what a hardy man he must be, and to not have a proper night's sleep for one night…"

Helen folded her arms tightly, glowering at her mother. "It was enough to lay me up in bed for days with a bad cold, Mama, and I was not fatigued from fighting off highwaymen and injured from a knife wound to the arm. He could be sick, his wound could be infected, he could have been attacked again, and he'd be all alone…" Her hand suddenly flew to her throat. "What if he's dying, Mama?"

Her mother shook her head, her brow furrowing. "That's the fastest I have ever seen you leap to conclusions, Helen, and I was there for your adolescence. What's driving you to all these extremes? You're not like this."

"I know, I know." Helen sighed and put her hands on her hips. "It's him."

"Jeremy?"

Helen nodded, tears rising yet again. "I just feel… abandoned. And foolish."

"He didn't abandon you, lamb," her mother assured her, coming to take her hands. "He's hiding from you, and from the shame of it all. Men do take things so very personally, love, but they can't always put words to it."

Helen shook her head slowly, a lump forming in her throat. "Oh,

Mama, I miss him so much. How can he leave me here after what we'd been through?"

Her mother pulled Helen into her arms, shushing her. "Because he probably loves you in return, and he probably did leave you with some indication, but given that he is a man of honor, whose honor is now in question because of the failure to protect you, he had no choice but to finish his task, and then ride off to right the wrongs."

That was impossible, Jeremy would never feel that way. And he hadn't done anything to make Helen feel even remotely hopeful.

Except for that warming brick.

And the blanket.

And that look in his eye.

And the kick to the shins.

Another rough exhale escaped Helen and her hand moved to her brow. "He loves me?" she asked, her voice breaking.

Her mother laughed and cupped her daughter's face. "I don't know, love. I don't even know who he is. But I think there is a definite reason to hope."

"Hope is all I've got," Helen told her. "And I don't even know that I really have that."

"Oh, Helen," her mother said with a much softer laugh. "Love is all about hope, especially when you don't know. Now," she paused as she straightened up almost stiffly, "what's this about you being foolish? I did not raise foolish children, aside from Elise, and we're working on that."

Helen coughed a surprised laugh and grabbed her mother's wrists. "Mama, you know I'm being foolish. It's obvious, isn't it?"

Her mother smiled and curved her fingers around Helen's hands. "No, darling, you are in love. But you are turning this all upside down and yourself inside out. That is only going to make you doubt everything and take all the fun out of it. This Jeremy fellow will come around, if he's the sort of man I think he is, and when he does, you will have to decide if you love him enough to believe his sincerity."

"I did believe him," Helen said softly.

"Did?" her mother repeated firmly. "Or do?"

Helen opened her mouth to reply, and yet there were no words to reply with.

Did she believe Jeremy? Did she believe that the man she had met in the coach, the one who was so much more than the man she had left London for, could possibly love her in return? Did she believe what he had said?

Everything I ever said to you or about you was the sincerest I've ever been in my life.

Her breath caught at the memory of his words. The look in his eye, the feel of his hand, the taste of his lips…

It had all been real.

She believed him.

And she believed *in* him, which seemed a rather more significant part.

Her mother saw the realization dawn on her, and Helen stared at her in wonder as she nodded. "What?" Helen asked.

Her mother shrugged with a knowing smile. "It seems you've reached a decision."

Helen grinned back at her. "I have."

"And?"

"I'm giving Jeremy two weeks," Helen told her as her mind whirled, and she felt life and energy seep back into her. "Just two weeks more, and if he isn't here in front of me, or hasn't sent some sort of word, I'll be in a coach back to London and taking him for myself."

Her mother laughed once and clapped her hands. "And if the gentleman doth protest?"

Helen grinned deviously, thinking of the Jeremy who'd whacked her across the shins in retaliation. "I'd like to see him try."

Chapter Thirteen

"Do you know, I think Rook might be ill."

"Do you really? I didn't know he was susceptible to such mortal afflictions."

"How else can we account for his solemnity and rather peaky expression?"

"He always looks like that."

"True, but he smiles more."

Jeremy looked up from his desk at Gent and Rogue, who leaned in the doorway to the office like bizarre mirror images of each other.

"With the pair of you standing there, I have nothing to smile about."

"Hmm," Gent hummed, tilting his head. "That was a bit weak."

Rogue shook his head in disgust. "Far, far below his usual caliber. I'm quite disappointed."

"That's because your life is disappointing," Jeremy muttered, lowering his eyes back to the paper before him, a very boring, tepid report from the Parkerton solicitor, which neither of these colleagues should know he was investigating.

Rogue, for one, might kill him for interfering.

Which was understandable, as he was not even mentioned in his cousin's will.

Pity, that.

He'd been back in London for a week now, but he'd made a point of avoiding the League offices. With all of the information on Trace he had collected, some of which had been downright shocking, he'd had no choice but to present himself to Weaver. He'd been working with him and Tailor directly as they sifted through the information. Anything that the League could take on, they still would, he had been reassured, but until the whole of the new evidence was properly analyzed and compared with what they already had, nothing could be assigned to anyone.

Jeremy rather thought that meant he was no longer going to be getting confidential information about his fallen comrade, which was a bit of a relief. Keeping secrets from spies was always harder than from everyone else, particularly when it was something they had taken so personally.

So, he was making use of himself in whatever way he could, namely with the more superficial details. Why had the next in line for the title of Lord Parkerton not been contacted to come take up the lands? Why the secrecy around Trace's death, or did the Shopkeepers know more than they were letting on?

Could they possibly have proof that Trace was alive?

If that were the case, why were they not mounting an expedition to retrieve him? They'd been on such missions dozens of times, and Jeremy had been involved in three or four himself when he'd worked for the Foreign Office. Rescue missions tended to be his favorite sort, as they were universally more dangerous, but twice as rewarding. And for an operative like Trace, they would have the absolute best at their disposal, should such an operation be mounted.

Trick and Thistle and a handful of other deep-seated operatives, who never took part in large operations, might have even been eager to take it on.

But no, they all sat in their usual positions, thinking the worst along with everyone else.

And only Jeremy was clued in on the fact that there might be another alternative.

Damned Shopkeepers and their damned secrets.

Spies really were the worst.

"He's not really reading whatever that is."

"He's absolutely daydreaming."

"But what about, I wonder?"

Jeremy looked up at them in derision, sliding his document under a pile of others, then folded his hands neatly on his desk. "It is impossible to read anything of importance with you nannies hovering, so by all means, come in and sit down, interrogate me to your heart's content, and then maybe I will accomplish something today."

Gent grinned at Rogue, who only shrugged, and then did as they had been invited, making a show of settling in.

Jeremy waited ever so patiently, tapping his thumbs against the worn wood of his desk. "There, gentlemen," he drawled, once they were settled, "now that you are quite comfortable, what may I assist you with?"

"He's so polite," Gent praised, sliding his glance to Rogue.

"It's annoying."

"So are you, but we keep quiet about it," Jeremy told him.

Rogue smirked. "You're too quiet, Rook, and it's suspicious."

"Am I?" Jeremy asked mildly. "And here I thought you wished for me to be more reserved in nature."

"I didn't say I wasn't enjoying it," Rogue shot back. "Only that it was suspicious."

"It is, rather," Gent allowed, sounding apologetic. "You've been back from York for some time now, if your manservant is to be believed, and yet…"

"I don't want to talk about York," Jeremy interrupted roughly, sitting back and folding his arms.

Gent sat back. "If reports are to be believed, you and Larkin held off an attack of several men, captured one, and interrogated him, and then sent him down here with contacts where he has been singing like a bird for anyone who asks. Quite a feat, all told. And yet you don't want to talk about it?"

Jeremy met his eyes calmly. "No."

Gent's brow furrowed at that. "I read the report, and Helen wrote Margaret that it was handled remarkably well. I am very grateful."

"I don't want your bloody gratitude, Gent," Jeremy snapped.

Rogue leaned back a little, eyeing Jeremy carefully. "Rook, I'm not interested in whatever seems to be going on in your personal life to make you do a weak imitation of myself, but if there is something Gent or I can do to knock some sense into you, we are available."

Jeremy looked at Rogue with some alarm. "You're offering to help me?"

"Technically, I offered to beat you," Rogue clarified, "which should help you."

"That's what I expected," he grumbled. "I feel so much better now."

Gent crossed his ankle over his knee. "Come on, Rook. Out with it."

Jeremy looked at him for a long moment, then sighed heavily. "I dropped my guard. On the trip to York, I forgot myself and my purpose. I should have been alert and actively watching for dangers. I knew the risks of that road; I had been fully briefed on it before I left. And still, we were attacked."

"You can't prevent highwaymen," Rogue pointed out. "You just have to deal with them."

"I know that," he replied bitterly. "But these men had no idea who Helen was. They weren't after Helen at all. They wanted me."

The others stilled as the admission settled on them, and Jeremy felt it weighing on him even more heavily. The pressure on his chest that never dissipated. The terror that woke him every night.

The guilt that would never leave.

"Helen was put into danger because of me," Jeremy told them, shaking his head. "Yes, I took care of it, and yes, she is safe and without injury, but…"

"But it could have been so much worse," Gent murmured, his eyes unfocused and staring at nothing.

Jeremy watched him for a long moment, wondering if the comment were supposed to be accusatory of Jeremy or a reminder of Gent's own demons.

He'd nearly lost Margaret once, and that event had somehow gotten lost amongst Jeremy's own memories.

Gent might be able to relate.

"I don't know how to rid myself of this guilt," Jeremy murmured before he could stop himself. "I know that, logically, I did everything I could. But every time I think back on it, I am convinced there was more I could have done, or should have done, and then she would never have been in any danger at all." He ran a hand over his face and exhaled. "I put her in danger. I did."

"No, I did."

Jeremy looked up at Gent in surprised, finding his colleague's expression hard on him. "How?"

"How?" Gent repeated with a snort. "Rook, I asked you to take her. I was so concerned about her being targeted because of her connection to me that it never occurred to me that you might be targeted instead. I put you both in danger."

Jeremy was shaking his head before Gent finished. "No, no, that's not…"

"It's really my fault," Rogue broke in, sounding almost raw in his admission. "I'm the one who got compromised, which leaked the rest of you, so if we're pointing fingers, just point them all at me."

"Stop!" Jeremy ordered them both, looking between them. "Just stop. Neither of you are to blame for Helen being attacked."

"Helen wasn't attacked," Gent pointed out. "You were. And you took care of it. Helen suffered a cold, and that is all." He smiled a little, shaking his head. "Believe me, she's seen much worse."

Jeremy glared at him, his throat burning. "Seen worse than masked men shooting at her? And then me climbing out of the coach and scrambling up the side to shoot as many of them as I could and then beating one off of his horse so I could chase another, stab that one with a bayonet, and then tackle him off of *his* horse to the ground, where I stabbed him again and punched him repeatedly? Really? Worse than that?"

Gent's eyes were wide, but he smiled still. "Well, when you put it like that…"

"I can't believe I missed that," Rogue grumbled, rubbing at his curls. "It sounds brilliant."

Jeremy snorted softly and leaned his head back against the chair. "I couldn't bear to look at her after that. I felt… ashamed. Mortified, really. But beyond that…"

"Bloody terrified," Rogue finished, his mouth curving a little.

Jeremy nodded, his head scraping the chair a little. He looked at the pair of them without reservation. "How do you live with the fear? Knowing you could lose everything important to you at any time?"

Gent shook his head, exhaling, but he kept Jeremy's gaze. "You do everything in your power to prevent it and make every moment last. You find a singular woman who can bear the danger and the unknown, and you cling to her with all your might. You fight harder so you can return to them, you take on more danger to protect them, and each victory is infinitely sweeter."

Rogue cleared his throat and sat forward. "You can't protect them from everything, but your life is more worth living because of them. I'm actually a far better operative now, because there is more at stake now."

"How's that?" Jeremy asked dubiously.

"Everything is done with precision," Rogue explained. "Less risks are taken, even if the danger is the same. I take everything more seriously. I'm less reckless, less headstrong, less…"

"Roguish?" Gent suggested with a grin.

Jeremy chuckled as Rogue scowled. "You're a better operative because you're afraid?"

"In a word," Rogue replied, "yes."

"Absolutely," Gent added, no longer teasing.

Neither of them was making any sense. How could anything be better with such vulnerability? With so much to lose, how could anyone go headlong into danger?

And yet, hearing them say those things struck a chord within him. Gent and Rogue could not have been more different as men, and as operatives, but on this they were in perfect harmony. They had both found love and happiness and hadn't lost a single stride in their work as spies because of it.

As it happened, they were better.

He'd seen it.

But did he believe it?

"I'd imagine it makes things more complicated," Jeremy said slowly, feeling the tension in his chest begin to unravel.

"Oh, it's utter chaos," Gent scoffed, waving a hand.

"I really don't know how sane I am anymore," Rogue added with a wince.

Jeremy rolled his eyes. "You're making it sound rather perfect, both of you."

Gent's suddenly knowing look stopped Jeremy's cynicism where it lay. "You're in love with Helen, aren't you?"

Rogue coughed in surprise. "Damn, Gent, I told you to ease into that."

Jeremy gaped at them, blinking suddenly feeling rather difficult. "You... How could you...?"

"Oh, please," Gent said dryly, a twinkle in his eyes. "You think I didn't know? Or see?"

"It was painful to watch," Rogue broke in.

Now Jeremy knew they were baiting him, lying to get a reaction. There was no possible way they could have known that...

"Did you really think I didn't know anyone else who could have escorted Helen to York?" Gent asked him, now grinning outright.

Jeremy's heart stopped in his chest. Gent knew? All the time? But Helen was his relation, and he ought to have come after Jeremy with a weapon of his choice for daring to have feelings for her, and yet he'd put them together on purpose?

"Why?" Jeremy finally asked in return. "Why would you do that?"

"Because Helen was miserable," Gent admitted without shame. "Margaret told me that you were the reason she was going to York in the first place. Well, Mr. Pratt was, anyway."

That made Jeremy wince and look away. "I didn't mean..."

"And you were getting annoying with your airs in public and irritability in private," Gent went on, running right over Jeremy's guilt. "So, putting the pair of you together seemed the perfect way to push you both into some sort of recovery, regardless of the direction."

Jeremy frowned at his colleague, then lifted just one brow. "You didn't have a preference as to which?"

Gent laughed once. "I'd prefer for Helen to be happy, but I would have settled for less downtrodden and determined to get over you."

"You think she'd be happy with me?"

Jeremy's low question smoothed Gent's brow and curved his mouth. "You don't?"

His breath caught and he felt as though he could fall sideways. Could Helen be happy with him? He'd be happy with her, blissfully so, and he thought he could treat her well, make her smile, or even laugh, but would that be enough? If he loved her every day with the fierceness he currently felt, gave up fighting against it, let himself be entirely himself with her… would it be enough to make her happy?

It seemed unfathomable, but… he thought it just might.

It honestly might.

"I love her, Gent," Jeremy admitted with more sincerity, and sheer honesty, than he'd ever admitted anything in his entire life. "And if I can manage it, I want to marry her."

Gent chuckled to himself. "I should hope so. And I doubt you'll have anything to say on the subject, if Helen has anything to do with it."

Jeremy managed a weak smile. "But it was such a whirlwind trip, Gent. Such a short time that we were actually together without any of the pretenses of Society, and I just don't know that… What if it's not enough time to know for certain?"

Gent raised a brow. "How much time did I spend with Margaret before I knew what I had been feeling was love?"

That was a fair point, and Jeremy considered it. Two days at most was all that Gent and Margaret had had, but Jeremy was convinced it had only been one before Gent had known.

Could the case be the same here?

He hadn't dared to hope before, but now…

Rogue snorted once. "I can't believe you're encouraging him to join your family."

Jeremy tossed a sardonic glance at him, feeling more himself than he had in days. "I'm perfectly lovable."

Gent shrugged. "Thankfully, I'm not the one who has to decide that."

"No, but really…" Rogue trailed off with a grimace.

"I'm very fond of Helen, Rogue," Gent scolded.

Rogue shuddered. "I'm not *that* fond of anybody."

Jeremy stared at Gent, smiling a little. "You… want me… to be with her?"

Gent nodded slowly. "If she wants you, and you want her, I want you both to be together." His dark eyes suddenly turned hard, and his jaw tightened. "But so help me, if you do anything to harm her or put her directly into danger in any way…"

"Yes, I know," Jeremy sighed, waving a hand, "you'll do away with me in an as yet undetermined manner, and no one will ever find the pieces of my body."

"Something like that," Gent replied with a grunt of satisfaction.

"Ooh, can I help?" Rogue inquired, brightening markedly.

Gent frowned at him. "You don't even care about Helen."

Rogue returned his look with an utterly superior one of his own. "Where Rook's destruction is concerned, I bloody adore Helen."

Jeremy barked a laugh and waved the pair of them out. "Away, both of you. No one is being romantic in any way today! I've got loads of reports, and so do you, and your stupidity is contagious."

They returned his jabs with well-placed barbs of their own, and he shook his head, finding the pair of them more ridiculous than he'd ever really dreamed.

But in the silence of his office, he played their words over and over in his mind. Never mind that Gent might approve of Jeremy as suitor for Helen, that was another matter entirely.

Could he make Helen happy when he was disappearing for weeks at a time and unable to tell her where he was going or why? She was a curious, intelligent, sensitive woman, and though she was strong and independent, she might object to being so often kept in the shadow of his secrets.

Images of Miss Edgewood in her mourning sprang into mind, and the warmth he had begun to feel dissolved all too quickly.

How could he do that to Helen?

How could he give her something that he couldn't promise would last? How could he leave her side, knowing it could be the last time he saw her? Every time he left, it could be the last. Agony at every parting. Fear at every moment. Aching for home constantly.

And there was no telling what Helen would feel.

If she felt for him even a portion of what he felt for her, it would be torment.

His first instinct had been correct. It had to be. He had to leave her, let her hate him, if she must, and then she could forget him and move on with her life. She could find someone else, someone who wouldn't put her in danger in any way. Someone who would only ever give her a life of joy.

Not him.

It was too risky to be with him.

Too painful.

Jeremy closed his eyes and groaned. He'd been so used to living his life without concern for anybody else, without having to think of consequences, without reservation, and now…

Now…

"You look like you are on the brink of a roaring headache."

Jeremy looked up to see Weaver in his doorway, and he nearly swore under his breath. "How do you always turn up here at inconvenient times?" he demanded of his mentor. "Do you have a key? A secret passage? Some sort of clairvoyance?"

Weaver grinned crookedly and pushed into the room, shutting the door behind him. "I'm a spy, Rook. I have all of those things, but I don't need them."

"You're a ruddy diplomat who is supposed to be all politeness and affability," Jeremy pointed out.

The taller man shrugged one shoulder and pulled out the chair Rogue had only recently vacated, turning it to the side and dropping himself in it. "They're not mutually exclusive."

Jeremy shook his head and dropped his pen again, not that he'd managed to use it. "To answer your question, yes, I am about to have a mighty fine headache. I've had one for days."

Weaver hummed once. "Helen?"

"How did you know about that?" Jeremy scowled at Weaver, wondering if he had any secrets at all anymore.

"Well, it was obvious, wasn't it?" Weaver replied, completely unruffled. "It was only a matter of time."

Jeremy dropped his head to the desk, moaning dramatically.

"And you thought you were so careful," Weaver teased. "But really, she's a lovely woman, why the headache?"

"I'm a spy," Jeremy informed him, not raising his head, keeping his voice muffled.

"So I've heard."

Now Jeremy raised his head, glaring at Weaver. "So, it's too dangerous."

Weaver gave him a surprised look. "Is it? Goodness, I should tell my wife. And Gent's wife. And Rogue's. And Cap's, Tailor's, Tumbler…" He hissed at that. "Ooh, Tumbler will be most upset."

Jeremy ground his teeth at that. "Your point, Weaver?"

"My point, Rook," he told him, looking very superior, if not scolding, "is that nothing about our lives or our work precludes us from family life, if that is what we want. We put protections in place, and it suffices, though there are rare disasters. But there are rare disasters with anyone in the world, working in covert operations or not. Do the military men avoid marriage and family because they could die in battle? Do the politicians remain bachelors because such a visible employment puts them at risk for assassination attempts? What about barristers? They make enemies faster than anyone. Or a dozen other professions. Yes, there will be secrets, but they are not shameful secrets. They are dangerous ones."

Weaver paused, swallowing once. "And while my wife may not know what danger I am heading into, she does know there is danger. She knows full well what I am doing every time I walk out the back door of our home rather than the front. Ours is a noble profession that receives no accolades, and our wives cannot boast of it amongst their friends, but if you think for one moment that my wife, or Beth, or Margaret, or Amelia ever complain about why we are doing what we do, then you underestimate the strength and character of the female sex, let alone those particular women." Then Weaver smiled just a little. "And some of them rather enjoy being married to surprisingly dangerous men. Mine in particular."

"Oh, lord," Jeremy muttered, smiling in spite of himself. "So, you're telling me to get over it and get on with it?"

Weaver nodded briskly. "More or less, yes. And I think Helen could be the making of you, Rook."

That surprised him, and he slowly leaned back against his chair, watching his mentor for a long moment.

She could be the making of him.

Well, of course she could. She was brilliant, challenging, vivacious, bold, tender, and…

And he loved every lovely inch of her, inside and out.

Being away from her made him ache and doubt everything he'd ever thought.

It tempted him to ride off to York and sweep her away to Gretna Green before he could think too long on it.

As well as a host of other things that left him breathless and tossed about, but there was a task at hand, and he was not nearly as impulsive as anybody thought he was.

Still, it was something to consider.

Jeremy cleared his throat and straightened. "So, what have we uncovered from Trace's files?"

Weaver smirked but took the diversion anyway. "A great deal, as it happens, which will not surprise you, as you found the hoard."

Jeremy nodded. He had figured as much, though he had not been involved in sorting it out, which irked him a great deal. "I want in on it."

Weaver laughed once. "Of course, you do. And you will be, once we have decided on a course."

"What do you mean, decided on a course?" Jeremy asked, drumming his fingers on the desk. "It should be fairly obvious, shouldn't it?"

"Not at all, actually," Weaver told him, his face a carefully guarded mask that Jeremy was all too familiar with. "We've had to bring in some different personnel to make heads or tails of over half of it, not to mention comparing it to what you, Rogue, and the others have sorted out since then. Despite being an ideal operative, Trace was surprisingly cryptic."

"He trusted no one," Jeremy grunted, looking out of the window. "Not his household, not his colleagues, not a soul. He knew the risks all too well and kept himself well guarded. Only he could understand the information, which ensured that it would never be compromised, if found, and he took great care that it could not be found easily."

"Which begs the question…" Weaver mused, a smile in his voice. "How did you find it?"

Jeremy smiled to himself. "Trace was a man in love, and I found myself able to understand that predicament quite well. It required thinking with the heart *and* the head, not just one or the other, and knowing Trace's wit, intellect, and proclivity for protection and secrecy, I ventured beyond the realm of the obvious, and found everything right in plain sight. Where everyone looking was sure to miss it."

The room was silent but for the soft ticking of the mantle clock on the sideboard.

"And you wonder why I brought you in on this," Weaver finally said with a soft laugh.

Jeremy glanced over at him, surprised by the proud smile Weaver wore. "What, because I have a new perspective?"

Weaver shook his head, still smiling. "No. Because you're very much like Trace, so you understand him. Even Rogue couldn't do that."

"That's because Rogue didn't have a heart until last year," Jeremy reminded him.

"You didn't see him when Trace died," Weaver said, the smile fading. "I thought we'd lose him after that. His grief and anger were unparalleled, and they blind him in this."

Jeremy hadn't considered that, and he was grateful at this moment that he hadn't witnessed that. "Whereas I have eyes wide open," he murmured.

Weaver dipped his chin, the solemnity abating somewhat. "In this, at least."

"Where am I blind?" he demanded with some indignation.

"I'd start a list, beginning with Helen Dalton, but I'd really rather be home at some point this evening," Weaver told him as he rose, heading for the door.

"You came all the way over here just to have this chat?" Jeremy laughed, rising as well.

The older man turned to face him. "Not quite. I came to tell you 'well done', and to see if you were free tomorrow evening."

Jeremy frowned. "Free for what? A social call?"

Weaver shook his head slowly. "We are bringing you in, Rook. To possibly reopen Trace's original investigation, to find out why they knew you were on the road to York, and to determine once and for all if Trace may yet be alive. With what you've uncovered, and what we already know, it's time."

Strength and stability left Jeremy's legs, and he pressed his hands into the desk to steady himself. "Why me?" Jeremy half-whispered. "Why not the others?"

"Honestly?" Weaver asked. "Because I can't bear to face any of them if we're wrong." He smiled faintly. "Tomorrow evening, Rook. It's going to be a rough road, and your only excuse for getting out of any of this will be if you're man enough to go after Miss Dalton."

Jeremy gaped after him as he swept from the room, chuckling softly to himself.

Man enough to...? He couldn't go after Helen...

Could he?

Chapter Fourteen

$\mathscr{H}$e could and he would and, dammit, if this report didn't wrap itself up this evening, he would curse Trace's memory until the end of time.

Another bleeding week in London, and he was at his wit's end.

Despite Weaver telling him that he would be excused if he went after Helen, Jeremy hadn't had time to consider doing anything of the sort, apart from when he was trying to sleep at night, which clearly kept him from sleep at night, which made Trace's cryptic reports to himself even more incoherent, which made Jeremy furious, which made everything worse.

But no more.

Tomorrow morning, he was riding off for York, and everything could wait.

Trace could wait, smugglers could wait, and the possibility of Jeremy's identity being compromised could bloody well wait.

Not that he wasn't concerned about all of those things, because he absolutely was.

But Helen couldn't wait.

And he was very much afraid that she wouldn't.

Still, there was too much to do to completely abandon things, and until he finished this, and finished it well, he could not, in good conscience, ride off to beg for the hand of his lady love.

And unfortunately, the investigation into Trace's affairs and delving into his case files was more comprehensive than anything Jeremy had ever been part of. He was barely keeping his head above the water with his responsibilities in the League on top of the rest of it, and keeping this all a secret from them was eating away at him slowly. This was their fallen comrade and friend, their cry for vengeance, and he couldn't let them know.

Couldn't give them relief.

Couldn't do anything to jeopardize the investigation, and with emotions running high due to yet more instances of compromised travels of contacts or operatives, he couldn't risk it.

He was alone in this, and it was a very hollow sort of feeling.

There ought to have been more answers with the number of people working through it, but everyone was being as careful and cautious as Jeremy was. There was almost no communication between anyone else unless they could be assured of security, and no one was taking any chances.

Jeremy trusted his comrades in the League, and their superiors, but anyone else was suspect. No conversations took place in open areas, even in code, and all of them were being tailed by trusted contacts for safety.

Even Gent's band of children were being diverted off of their usual tasks for much safer ones.

Everything was tense and uncomfortable these days, and a nagging sense of suspicion pervaded amongst the office, and within Jeremy's mind.

As far as any of them could tell, their public personas and real identities were still intact. There had been the scare with Rogue earlier in the year, and certainly with Cap, but measures had been taken with both of them to ensure it was less likely to occur again, and nothing had led them to believe the rest of them were similarly at risk. But if they could not get a handle on this, they would have to shut down the League and reassign them to one of the other offices.

Jeremy couldn't let that happen.

He'd loved his days with the Foreign Office, certainly, but this was something different. This particular group, who answered only to the Shopkeepers themselves, was above and beyond anything he'd ever been a part of. Now he was tasked with ferreting out where the discrepancy had been in Trace's work that had exposed his investigation and left him in danger. Everything seemed to trace back to it, and yet there was no sign that he had been aware of the problem.

Trace had been just as ignorant of the danger as they were now, and it had led to his death.

With all that Jeremy had to be getting on with, and with all that he had focused on Trace in the last few months, that thought terrified him.

And despite what Weaver had said about bringing him in on the investigation, he still knew only what he was permitted to know, not the whole of the picture, and it was maddening.

He'd been the one to find Trace's cache of intelligence and reports; why should he not be leading the investigation and putting more pieces together? Even his brother had a more integral part in this investigation than Jeremy did, and while John, in his work as Sphinx, was an utter genius with puzzles and codes and analysis, he wasn't tied to this in any way. And he almost never went out into the field, which meant the implications of much of the details he was sifting through would not relate to him.

Which, now that Jeremy considered it, was probably why Sphinx and the other intellects had been brought in.

And still, in the midst of all this madness, Jeremy found himself dwelling on Helen more than he ought to have done.

Lord, but he missed her.

It was strange, but those few days together had meant more to him than the full year of shameless flirtation they'd engaged in. Such a short amount of time where they had truly been themselves, but the condensed period had had an irrevocable effect on him. His future was no longer his, but theirs. Aspirations he'd had for years were now but a faint memory, and all he truly wanted in his life was her. A lifetime with her was his dream beyond dreams.

He was mad for her, mad for wanting her, and mad for staying away from her, but all of that would change tomorrow when he could, at last, set off for her.

It had taken days to settle on that course, which seemed ridiculous, as the way was quite clear before him, but he would admit that his concerns had been significant ones, and as such had required all due consideration. His colleagues had been no help at all in that quarter, as every instance they saw him was accompanied by an exclamation of disbelief that he was still there.

He was taking great care to avoid being seen for that particular reason.

Not that they were wrong, but because he knew he would have done the same.

And had done.

But had he truly understood what they must have endured, feeling what they did for their wives before they were claimed as such, and making sense of it all, he might have teased a little less and minded his own blasted business.

That made him snort softly to himself now. He ought to have known himself better than to suggest that he would choose to take less enjoyment out of plaguing his colleagues over matters of the heart just because he now could sympathize more. If anything, had he experienced it at the time, he might have done more to plague them.

And if he were to be perfectly honest with himself, which he rarely was, but seemed keen to be lately, he would admit that he was afraid.

Afraid it was already too late.

Afraid he had missed his chance.

Afraid that what he'd done was unforgivable.

Afraid…

Well, afraid she didn't want him in return, when it came down to it.

Jeremy Pratt was used to facing all sorts of fear and acting despite it, but this seemed to be an exception.

Some brave and daring man he was!

He slid the mostly finished report aside and shoved the entire collection of papers into the secret drawer of his desk, locking it soundly. There was no sense in attempting to make sense of any of this when Helen, and the pain of being without her, was dominant in his mind.

Helen reigned supreme for him in all things.

He put his face in his hands and sighed heavily. Tomorrow needed to be now, or he would go mad.

"I'd ask what you are doing in London, but I've already heard."

Jeremy dropped his hands in surprise as Cap's voice rang in his ears, and he stared at his superior and colleague in confusion. "I didn't know you were here, either."

Cap smiled a little, and the relatively new sight still took some getting used to after years of knowing him. "Just arrived." He pushed into the room, looking pristine in eveningwear, which was not usual for the offices, despite Cap's station in life.

Jeremy eyed him pointedly. "On your way to a party, or just escaped one?"

"On my way," Cap replied easily, not sitting. "And so are you."

"No, I am not," Jeremy told him, gesturing to the mountains of paperwork, not that he'd been working on any of those. "As you can see, Rook is staying in."

Cap's lips quirked. "Rook has an assignment tonight, because Mr. Pratt is needed at Lady Blackmoor's ball."

Jeremy shook his head. "No, I think you'll find Mr. Pratt isn't in London at present. He's heading for York, as it happens."

"Not until tomorrow."

Jeremy stared at Cap in horror, though he really should have known better. "How did you know that?"

The question seemed to amuse Cap. "You informed Weaver you would be unavailable tomorrow, and he told me. And I know perfectly well why, and I approve of the trip."

"Oh, good," Jeremy muttered with a scowl. "My secrets have the approval of everybody I work with now."

Cap tilted his head. "Really? I didn't know One and Two had any insight on the matter."

The mention of their code names for the poor clerks who worked with them made Jeremy snort. "They're about the only ones who don't know, and I'd be very surprised indeed if they haven't heard, as well." He looked up at Cap again. "Did you bring Beth to London? Or is this just business?"

Cap smiled at his wife's name. "No, I brought her. She's feeling quite well, so we've come to London for a few days. You'll have to fawn her appropriately when we get there, she's looking forward to Mr. Pratt bemoaning her married state."

Jeremy almost smiled but shook his head. "And I would do her justice, believe me, but I am in no mood for a ball."

"You seem to be under the impression that you have a say in this."

There was no arguing with Cap when he took on that tone, and Jeremy thought to try for one more argument. "I'm not ready for a ball, Cap. Not as Mr. Pratt, and not as myself."

Now Cap smiled in earnest, which was downright alarming. "I surmised as much. So, I've brought reinforcements." He whistled once, and a pair of crisp footsteps could be heard from the front of the offices.

"I do so hate being whistled at. It gives quite the wrong impression," came a voice that Jeremy knew too well, and he groaned at hearing it.

Tilda appeared in the doorway, rather grandly attired, her arms full of equally exquisite garments, and her dark hair and eyes twinkled merrily. She was one of their favorite contacts and assets, a costumer extraordinaire in the theaters of London, and one of the more terrifying women Jeremy had the acquaintance of.

"Hello, darling," Tilda cooed, crooking a finger at him. "I've been wanting to get my hands on you for ages. It's like Christmas and my fourth wedding all at once."

Cap coughed a laugh and stepped out of the way as Jeremy trudged over to her.

There was no arguing with Tilda, and a ball could prove a useful distraction. Or it would make him miss Helen even more, which would only spur him on faster to reach her in the morning and make his argument more ardent.

So, perhaps being trussed up by a costumer before his superior would be worth it.

And Tilda did tend to have excellent taste in garments.

He let her have her way with his clothing, then agreed to bring her to the ball on his arm under the guise of being his cousin Alice, which ought to provide him with necessary entertainment, and Cap quite tired of the pair of them before they ever rolled up to the Blackmoor's residence in the rather subdued Montgomery crested coach.

But Lady Blackmoor was very polite and warm, greeted them affably, and smirked at Jeremy in a way he wasn't sure he cared for.

He'd never interacted with her much, but he knew from others that she was a very mischievous, lively woman when she had a mind to be, and he thought he recollected Gent rushing off with her husband to save her at some time or another.

Odd that she should find his presence tonight amusing.

Lord Blackmoor didn't look pleased about anything, unless he was looking at his wife, but that was to be expected.

'Cousin Alice' wandered away from Jeremy almost at once, which defeated the purpose of having her come with him, and Jeremy shook his head as he swiped a cup of punch from a nearby table.

"For heaven's sake, Monty," he grunted to Cap, careful not to spill punch on his gold-striped waistcoat, "why did I let you bring me to this sad assembly?"

Cap inclined his head politely, expression sober, eyes oddly filled with mirth. "Because Lord Marlowe insisted I do so, and I found his reasoning to be exceptionally good." He bowed and moved across the room to his beautiful, charming, rather delighted-looking wife, leaving Jeremy to fend for himself.

"Traitor," he muttered, sipping his punch.

Then Cap's words sank in.

Lord Marlowe insisted that Mr. Pratt attend? Why in the world would Gent do any such thing, and why in the world would Cap listen to anything Gent suggested where Society was concerned? It was the most absurd thing Jeremy had ever heard.

He looked around the room, doing his best not to frown, as Mr. Pratt never frowned in public, scanning every face and figure for a sign of Gent or Margaret. They were going to be questioned as to motives and intent and…

His heart caught in his chest as another sight met his eyes, brilliant and beautiful, swathed in a breathtaking blue, and staring at him with marked intensity.

Helen was here.

The moment Jeremy's eyes met hers, Helen wanted to smile.

Not just a soft, sultry, inviting smile, but an all-out beaming grin that hid absolutely nothing about her feelings at this particular moment.

Two full days she had waited in London for this, all the while listening to Rafe telling her to be patient, though he was the one who had written her in York and given her reason to race to London as fast as she could.

"Get to London," his letter had told her. "There's a lovesick man who thinks he can't have you moping about, and it is really quite sad."

She'd departed two days later, though she'd been planning to stay another day or so beyond that. Her parents had accompanied her, with an additional escort of three riders, who looked suspiciously similar to the ones that had ridden up with her and Jeremy, one of whom had been ever-present when she needed to leave the grounds at Leighton.

It made no difference. They had arrived without incident, and she had been dying of the anticipation of seeing Jeremy again.

And now she had… and she couldn't move.

She stared at him, and he stared at her, and the only thing she was aware of was the blood pounding in her ears at a very steady cadence, strangely not at all racing.

He was dressed as elaborately as Mr. Pratt ever had been, but she could see past that now. Those eyes staring at her with a raw need belonged entirely to Jeremy.

Her Jeremy.

Suddenly, it was all worth it. Driving Margaret and her mother mad with her indecision over gowns hours ago, thumping along in a coach with her parents for London despite having just made the journey, even her misery at Leighton over being without him was all worth it.

Just to see him again, and to see him like this.

There were no more questions, no more doubts. When he looked at her like that, she knew everything she needed to.

And Helen Dalton was quite done with waiting one moment longer.

"Go," Margaret whispered from behind her. "Don't just stand

there, go!"

Helen heard Rafe shush her, say something about ten seconds, and the pair of them snickered to themselves, but Helen paid them no mind.

She wasn't waiting at this moment.

She was watching.

She watched Jeremy take in every inch of her. She watched his throat work. She watched his hands fidget as his sides.

But when his chest moved on a deep, unsteady exhale, she moved.

Slowly, pointedly, she made her way around the room, skirting the edge of the dancing, never taking her eyes off of his. She heard scant whispering as she approached him, and she hoped the gossips enjoyed this.

She knew she would.

Jeremy's eyes darkened to a deeper green than she'd expected, and he exhaled roughly when she reached him. "Lord, Helen..." he breathed.

She let herself smirk at that. "Quite so, Mr. Pratt." She tossed her expertly set hair and quirked a brow at him. "I noticed that you didn't have a dance reserved with me this evening, is that something you would like to remedy?"

Jeremy's slow, heated smile made her toes curl in her beaded slippers. "Yes. I want all of your dances. Until the end of time."

Be still her fluttering heart...

"Are you sure?" she asked, somehow managing a flirtatious tone. "I can be quite a handful."

He nodded once, his smile turning tender. "I'm always sure, Helen. I want whatever trouble you cause, and all of the messes you create." He swallowed and took a step forward, reaching for her hand. "I love you, and I'll always be sure of that, too." He drew her hand up and kissed the inside of her wrist, though the skin was covered by her long, white gloves.

The fabric made no difference. The heat from his lips raced up her arm and into her chest, catching her breath almost painfully.

"Lord, Jeremy..." she whispered shakily, smiling more naturally for him.

He returned it. "Just Jeremy will suffice."

Helen burst into fits of laughter and reached for his coat with her free hand to steady her. "Oh, I love you."

He settled a hand on her elbow, pressing the hand he held against his heart, and leaning almost improperly close. "If that is so, then I need you to find your father so I can ask for your hand."

Helen scoffed without shame and kicked his shins gently. "Ask *me*, you dolt. Papa won't care one way or another, so long as I am happy."

Jeremy chuckled and pointedly tapped his foot against her skirts. "Will you be my wife, Helen Dalton?" he asked softly, brushing his nose against hers. "Would that make you happy?"

She sighed in delight and moved her hand to cup his face. "Yes, Jeremy. And yes… it very much would."

"You sure?" he pressed, stroking the fingers he still held. "I have… a great many secrets."

She nodded, drumming her fingers along his cheek. "I know."

He leaned back a little, mildly surprised. "You do?"

"Well," she laughed easily, "I don't know your secrets, but I do know you have them."

"And that doesn't bother you?" He seemed almost uncertain, though she could sense his budding excitement.

Helen smiled at him, her heart ready to burst into flame or song or both. "No. You can have your secrets, so long as I can have you. The real you." Her lower lip began to tremble, and she bit it softly. "Because I am sure of you still, Jeremy Pratt. And I always will be."

Jeremy held her gaze for a long moment, then sighed with some pain. "Lord, but I want to kiss you right now."

"Dance with me," Helen urged, pulling him towards the others. "Surely a man with your talents can sweep us away unnoticed at a convenient time."

He grinned mischievously, squeezing her hand. "He most certainly can, and I most certainly will."

They moved into the dance easily, shocking no one, and gracefully taking part, just as any other couple might have done, though they did seem to garner more looks and attention than they usually did.

Helen could not have cared less about that. Her feet could not dance any more than her heart already was, nor could the music lift her any higher than her soul already flew.

Jeremy's eyes never left her, even when the dance parted them, and Helen felt her cheeks begin to slowly heat under his intensity. And she was going to marry this man? She'd be nothing but embers the rest of her days.

And lord, what a time that would be.

"How are you here?" Jeremy finally asked. "By what magic are you here this evening? I was coming to you in the morning, all the way to York, but here you are."

"It was Marlowe, not magic," she replied with a laugh. "He told me there was a lovesick chap bemoaning the loss of me, and that I ought to see to it. Any idea where I might find him?"

Jeremy laughed back, shaking his head. "I have a few ideas, but we may have to save those for another time." He wrenched his gaze from her to glare at Rafe, who only raised a glass, looking so bored it was amazing he was not asleep on his feet.

"Marlowe is a very interfering man," Helen informed Jeremy primly.

"You have no idea," came the muttered retort.

She grinned at hearing it. "That, and I found the man you hired to mind me while I was in York, and he all but slept outside my room." She raised a brow, delighted to have found out his plan.

If her discovery surprised Jeremy, he did not show it. And in fact, he looked quite pleased with himself. "I would have told him to do so, if I thought it necessary."

Helen let herself sigh, smiling gently at the man she adored above all others. "Jeremy, there is only one man I ever want to sleep outside of my room, and it's the same man I want to sleep inside of my room, and that man is you."

The dance came to an end, and Jeremy bowed over Helen's hand, his eyes still on hers. "Far be it from me to refuse my lady love." He pressed his lips to her knuckles. "Now, shall we see about sneaking away so I might kiss you for a good long while before being properly presented to your parents as your new intended?"

"New intended?" Helen repeated as he pulled her away.

"Whatever happened to my old intended if you are the new?"

"Don't know, don't care," Jeremy retorted as his pace quickened. "But I highly doubt he kicked your shins the way I do."

"Nobody kicks my shins the way you do," she informed him, dipping her voice for his benefit.

An empty corridor obtained, Jeremy turned around and pressed her into the wall, his perfect lips curving all too perfectly. "Too right, Miss Dalton," he murmured as his hand moved to her face, his thumb stroking her cheek. "And nobody will."

"Tell me one secret, Jeremy," Helen breathed as her skin tingled. "Just one."

He stroked her cheek again. "I'll tell you as many as I can, love. But for now, just one." He exhaled shortly. "I'm a spy. For the Crown."

She stared at him for a long moment, the various pieces falling into place as Jeremy Pratt finally became a whole and complete picture in her mind. Suddenly, everything about him made perfect sense.

And she loved him even more.

"Oh," she half moaned, half gasped. "I heartily approve, Jeremy."

Jeremy smiled at that. "You do, do you?"

She nodded against the wall. "Yes."

His eyes crinkled at the corners and he leaned closer. "You like that secret?"

"I like that secret," she agreed, nodding once more. "Very much."

"Then here's another," he whispered, bringing his lips to her ear. "I adore you beyond measure, Helen Dalton. And I've missed you."

She shivered at the contact, and more at the words, and sighed as she sank fully against the wall. "That's no secret, darling," she whispered back. "I already know."

Jeremy kissed her then, his lips hungry and tender and easily unraveling her strand by strand.

And nothing else was said, or needed to be, for quite some time.

But once or twice, Helen did tap his shins.

And he always tapped back.

Epilogue

"It was a lovely wedding, Rook. Truly, we all enjoyed it immensely."

"Speak for yourself. I hate weddings."

"That's not what you said when you were weeping."

"I'm not sure weddings are meant to be enjoyed by the men," Jeremy mused as he leaned against the bookcase, swirling his glass of brandy, unable to keep from smiling.

"Now that, I agree with," Rogue said with a nod as he sipped at his own brandy. "I won't say I minded my own wedding, but it is rather a lot of fuss, isn't it?"

Gent laughed shortly. "Fuss, was it? To make vows before God and in the eyes of the law about taking a woman as your own flesh for the rest of your days and she doing the same for you? Yes, that should be a much simpler affair."

Cap chuckled and looked remarkably at ease in the wingback chair he sat in. "Well, when put that way, I suppose it should have more pomp."

"No," Rogue grunted. "Not even a little, Cap."

Jeremy smiled, his eyes moving to the door, just beyond which, his bride was mingling with the few guests they had been able to coerce back to London so long after the Season had ended.

It had been a full five weeks since their engagement, which was longer than usual, but for some reason, Lady Riverton had insisted on seeing to Helen's trousseau along with Mrs. Dalton, and so the fuss had gotten in the way of a timely ceremony by usual Society standards.

Jeremy hadn't minded, especially not now that Helen was his wife. Not now that he felt full to the brim with all the joy and contentment in the world.

There hadn't been anything wanting in his life before this, but at the moment, he felt as though there had been a void that was now filled.

"Oh, look at that smile," his brother drawled, his teasing tone an unusual one for him. "One would think he's besotted."

"Think?" Gent laughed, clapping John on the back. "He's more far gone than any of us ever were!"

Jeremy turned to look at the roomful of men and bowed a little. "And gladly do I accept such a title, and more gladly will I wear it. My wife will be more envied than any of yours for having such a husband, and you'll all spend the rest of your days desperately trying to match us."

They all laughed at that, though Rogue's was in derision.

Having seen Rogue and Amelia together, there was a fair bit of competition there. Actually, all of them were shockingly devoted to their wives, and it would be a struggle to match any, let alone surpass them.

Well, except for John.

"And now we just have to find a bride for Sphinx," Jeremy pointed out as he sipped his beverage once more.

His brother skewered him with a cold look as the others all rounded on him.

Jeremy knew better. If John married, it would surprise both of them. He was too reserved and reclusive, and any wife of his would have to measure up to his intellect and let him have that reserve.

There weren't many of those, as far as they knew.

Helen had already decided to put her mind to it, and John was properly warned, but he liked Helen so much that he might permit her interference.

To a point.

"Where did Fritz get to?" Cap asked aloud as he rose with a groan. "I know he was here, we sat by him and Lady Rothchild."

"Not sure," Jeremy admitted, looking out the door. "He said he'd... Oh, here he is now."

Weaver approached the study with determined steps, eyes lowered, his face set.

Jeremy's stomach dropped, and his mind raced. He couldn't have anything disastrous on his wedding day. He couldn't. He needed this day for Helen, for both of them, some time to just be before the danger in his life reached him again.

Weaver gave no indication of his thoughts as he entered the room, but he lifted his eyes to them all and shut the door softly behind him.

"Weaver?" Cap prodded, his tone formal and businesslike, while the rest of them stood almost at attention.

Weaver stared at him a long moment, then looked over at Jeremy. "I am sorry to do this on your wedding day, Rook, but word has just reached me, and I don't know when the next opportunity would be to share this."

"Share? Share what?"

The entire room seemed to hold its breath, eyes fixed on this particular Shopkeeper, one of their leaders, and the one who seemed almost one of their own at times.

Weaver exhaled, swallowed, then raised his chin.

"Trace is alive."

Coming Soon

The London League
Book Five

"Nothing but a trace remains..."

by

Rebecca Connolly

More Romance from Phase Publishing

by
Emily Daniels

Devlin's Daughter

Lucia's Lament

A Song for a Soldier

by
Laura Beers
The Beckett Files

Saving Shadow

A Peculiar Courtship

To Love a Spy

A Tangled Ruse

A Deceptive Bargain

The Baron's Daughter

by
Grace Donovan
The Saints of Laredo

Saint's Ride

CPSIA information can be obtained
at www.ICGtesting.com
Printed in the USA
LVHW081945290520
656948LV00010B/760

9 781943 048847